When a dating app matches two serial killers, they find them-
selves falling into love — or the closest thing that their twisted
minds can get. Desperately trying to keep their secret crimes
from being exposed, they must deal with not only each other
but law enforcement and the demands of their careers. Will
they overcome the odds and accept that they are meant for
each other?

Slash Right
Copyright © 2020 Myra Flexion
ISBN: 978-1-4874-2991-1
Cover art by Martine Jardin

Published by eXtasy Books Inc or
Devine Destinies, an imprint of eXtasy Books Inc

Look for us online at:
www.eXtasybooks.com or www.devinedestinies.com

Slash Right

By

Myra Flexion

DEDICATION

Dedicated to the ones who thought they'd be single forever. Hang in there, and hide the bodies well.

CHAPTER ONE

I love the smell of the city after a summer rain.

Normally, the city smells of sweat and car exhaust and concrete baking in the Midwestern sun. It's hot and humid and mean, and it grinds you down until you flee to the air conditioning and the cold metal seats of all the little cafes and eateries scattered across downtown like hidden, cool diamonds.

Those are nice. But eventually, you have to go outside, and it's rough, and it grates on you and makes you hide from the sun again.

But when it rains . . . when it rains, there's this coppery smell, this electric smell that dances through the salt in the air and makes the mist rise from the sidewalks.

I stand there on the balcony, letting my bare breasts rest on the railing, looking out into the secret yard, the alley between buildings. A few homeless men huddle there, but they aren't looking up, have no reason to look up. The rain's keeping their heads down, eyes closed.

I flip open his wallet and count the money. I'll stop by later and give them some. This is their city, too, and nobody really looks at them, nobody wants to help.

I turn and glance back toward the bedroom. "Have you ever really thought of the homeless before?"

There's no reply.

I stretch. My muscles got a workout the night before. It was a good time. Dinner was *exquisite,* and afterward, ah . . . that was divine.

I needed that.

I close the window, shutting out the electric smell. But it still smells coppery in a different way. Warm copper, not hot. Sweet copper, not salt.

I track down where I threw my clothes last night. Yellow skirt, knee-length. Black halter top, spaghetti straps. A short, black leather jacket. A pair of pumps, scuffed where I tripped on the sidewalk last night. I wasn't nearly as drunk as he thought I was. Otherwise, he wouldn't have dared, and we wouldn't have ended up here.

His clothes are scattered around, too, and in his back pocket, I find the wedding ring.

"I knew," I whisper to the ring, and I lick it, tasting that salt, the fever salt of a cheating man way out of his depth.

Then I slide it on my finger. Not where it belongs, but it isn't like I'll ever know the feel of one made for *me*.

Dressed, now. Sporty! One last sweep . . . did I bring underwear this time? No, no, I did not. Damn the pants! Full speed ahead!

Then my purse, and the sample kit as well. A briefcase, heavier than it looks.

That's fine. I'm stronger than I look, too.

And then the micro-fridge, and the paper-wrapped packages that crinkle with the plastic inside. My mouth fills with saliva as I put them carefully in the sample case. No leaking!

One last sweep through the suite, checking the shower for hair, making sure I didn't leave anything behind, and then it's back to the door to the bedroom, and that rich, warm coppery smell floating through the air. I can almost see the clouds of it, can almost taste it on the back of my tongue, like I did last night.

"Goodbye, love," I tell him. And I take *her* from the doorknob where she hung all night, watching over him. Into my purse she goes, the leather layers folding up along well-worn creases.

There's more I can do, but I learned not to worry about it long ago. Things work out.

And it's a beautiful day!

The stairway down smells of old drugs and new cleaning products, and I clutch my purse tighter. The security door opens directly onto the street, and I let the rain wash down on me. It's going to do a number on my hair, and I should have brought a hat, but oh well. I pull my jacket tighter around me and start the walk home.

People call this part of town dangerous, but it's not, not really. I look like a lot of the women who walk these streets here. I look like I belong. And it's raining, too. Nobody who's looking to hassle people comes out in the rain without a really good reason. Nobody brings me down as I splash through puddles until I get to High Street. Then a turn, and I start the long walk to the Short North.

Midway through, the rain picks up, and even I'm starting to get a little annoyed. There are comfy and yummy smells, and then there's getting soaked to the bone. I pull out my phone, and it's his, instead.

For a second, I'm worried, a lance of cold dread in my stomach, and I fumble around . . . ah, there's my phone. I turn his off, yank the battery, and dump it down a storm drain. I shield mine from the rain as best I can, and my fingers glide across the screen. *Uber* time!

The SUV pulls up five minutes later, and I get in with a grateful smile.

The driver takes a moment to check me out in the mirror. "You all right, lady?" He's a few years younger than me — late twenties, perhaps, with black-rimmed round glasses and a hipster beard.

I give him the biggest smile I've got. "I am, thanks! Got caught in the rain."

"Sorry to hear it," he says, and the *Ford Explorer* heads off into traffic. I settle back into the seat and relax. The air conditioning in here is fresh, with a hint of pine . . . probably due to that cardboard tree swinging from the mirror.

His gaze plays over me at the traffic stops, and I pretend not to notice. But it is funny to watch his eyes flicker when he catches sight of the wedding ring. "I'm surprised you didn't call your husband to come get you."

"It didn't work out. We're not together anymore," I tell him. Technically true.

"Sorry to hear it."

"Don't be. He had issues." Also technically true.

"You doing anything Sunday?"

Well! This one doesn't waste time!

"Sorry. It's too soon," I say, and it *is*. I'm going to be floating for the rest of the day. Maybe tomorrow, too. This was a *good* one.

"Right, uh, sorry I said anything."

"Don't be! You're sweet." He apologized, and that's no small thing. More than the standard hipster. "What's your name?"

"Chris Devon."

"Two first names?"

Chris grins, making his beard flex against his neck, and now we're pulling up by my place. "I've got a card in the seatback pouch. If you ever want to talk or need another ride, I don't mind a text or three."

He might be just my type. I take a card and take a second to do the *Uber* payment thing and leave a middling-sized tip.

I click my card into the slot and enter the building. Stale air conditioning hits me, but once I get into my own place, it's tolerable. The array of open-jarred spices, the incense stick I set burning last night . . . all of these blend into the same scent.

Home.

I open the sample case and check to make sure the

packages didn't leak. My fingers rest on the brown paper, and I crinkle it a bit, remembering the good times last night. Each package goes in the refrigerator after I make a little room for them next to the fresh chicken I got from the poultry farm two days ago. It's next to the gourmet selection gouda cheese that I got at the North Market last week . . . probably still good, but I should eat it soon.

It's been a while since I had friends over. Why eat alone?

Work first, though.

Off come the club clothes and on go my business duds — no-nonsense granny panties, a simple bra, and a pastel pink blouse and slacks over them. A white suit jacket matches with the white dress shoes and some simple makeup covers the face.

The wedding ring goes on the dresser. I'll deal with it later.

The knives come out of the sample case and into the dishwasher. New knives go into the case from my last order. I check my phone scheduler to make sure the next meeting is when and where I thought it was.

I head down to the side lot, get my little pink *VW Bug* out of its parking spot, and take off toward Easton. Traffic's not bad at eight in the morning . . . almost everyone's at work by now. A hop and a skip down the highways, a quick stop for gas, and I'm over in Easton.

"Hey, Sauro," I say as I head into the doors of the Cucina Sicilia, and the smells of garlic and parmesan and sun-dried tomatoes wash over me. "We got a good crowd today?"

"Bambina!" Sauro cries and rushes out from behind the counter. "Mi Piccoletta!" His meaty arms fold around me, and I giggle as I hug him back. He swings me around a few times, then sets me on the ground with a grunt. "Ah, this is getting harder! I'm getting old, a Jenny."

I'm never Jenny or Jenn or Jennifer with him. It's always *a Jenny*. But that's fine. It's one of the little things that makes

Sauro who he is. It goes along well with his fat, beloved wife and their big Catholic family.

All of these things make him one of the *good* ones.

She will never see him.

"This crowd, she's glorious! Magnifico!" He kisses his hand, and I giggle again. "You gonna sell all the knives!"

He's happy. He's already made his cut. It's thirty dollars a seat to get in, and I see precisely none of that. But I don't care, because that's his money, not mine. And it's not about the money, no.

It's about walking in and tossing my suit jacket to the left, knowing that Amy will catch it and seeing fifty happy faces light up as they cheer for me. It's about not knowing which recipe I'll be doing today, as I see the ingredients laid out on the bar, and the cuts of meat ready for the slicing all in their neat little white porcelain trays.

"All right!" I yell back to the cheering crowd, mostly women, mostly middle-aged, all thrilled to be here. "Who's ready to go *chopping?*"

That's my catchphrase. That makes everybody go wild. I hop up on the stepstool that lets me get the height I need over the counter, plop my sample case in the luggage holder waiting at just the right angle, and draw out the *Mark 4 Chopco Butcher's Knife.*

It's a fabulous knife. *She* tested one just like it last night. It worked great!

And oh boy, do I get a good slice as I roll out a tomato, pin it to the cutting board, and bring the butcher's knife down with a meaty *chonk.* No juice spray at all! Clean through, and it was a firm tomato, to begin with.

I point these facts out to the enthralled audience, gesturing with the knife at the juice dribbling onto the cutting board. Then I squint to make out the chalkboard across the way. "Okay, so today's recipe . . . Amy, what've we got here?"

My eyesight isn't great, but I can't wear glasses. I started this livestream without glasses, and I don't know how it'll affect my numbers if I wear them.

But it's Amy to the rescue, as always. "Chicken Penne Al Fresco!"

"Does it have tomatoes?" I ask her, drawing a laugh from the audience.

"Yes, but . . . it calls for grape tomatoes. Not the big ones."

"Screw it! My version does!" I say, and I pull out three tomatoes, rolling them across the cutting board and whacking each one into halves. The crowd laughs. I love it, and I grin back. "We're hacking the recipe! No waste! Not now, not never!"

The sound of cardboard waving through the air and a stiff breeze stirring my hair tells me that Amy is waving the *Double Down* sign.

This is one of my tricks. I get into a recipe, get something wrong, and instead of trying to correct it, we carry on regardless. Substituting tomatoes is pretty easy as it goes, but not every show has to be complicated.

I use the cleaver mostly, dicing the chicken and the tomatoes before I start combining all the ingredients. Some of the red wine goes into me instead of the recipe, and they laugh at that, too. I don't stop talking for more than a few seconds as I work.

And when it goes in the oven, I wave my hands, now empty of knives. "Okay, everyone! Check under your chairs!"

Fifty people scramble out of their chairs, and there's a minor scuffle as the people lifting chairs up try to avoid braining the people who are crouching down. I stifle a giggle of my own . . . I'm small, and perhaps there was a bit too much red wine. No, no, that's not it. I'm still riding the high from last night.

Wow, I'd needed that.

It's all the better . . . but it won't last. But that's a worry for tomorrow, or the next day, or the day after that, if my strange brain is merciful for once.

A figure comes up from under his chair, squealing with joy, and it's a man for once. But from the tone of his voice and the way he's dressed, I don't think he's a bad one. No, no, that's his boyfriend or husband hugging him now. So cute!

He comes up with the heart-shaped token, and I give him a big hug and air kisses, which he happily returns. "First time on the show?" I whisper. He's not a tall man, but I have to stand on tiptoes to whisper near the vicinity of his ear.

"Oh, yes! We're longtime watchers, though! We were in town from Pennsylvania, and oh my god, this is *fabulous!*"

"Hahaha! Lucky! Wellp, come on, then!" I pull out the stool for him, and he hops up on it. His name is Peter, and we chat about this and that and everything and nothing, and he has the most amazing nails. He had them done here in town, and I spend a few minutes hunting down the salon on my phone and plugging them for the stream. Amy will call them later and let them know they got a boost. She'll ask to put up a few ads for the show in their shop in return. It's how we roll.

Ten minutes later, the timer dings, and I dig my dish out of the microwave. I sprinkle the cheesy-basil-y mix on it just like the recipe calls for, and I share it with Peter. It's pretty good. Didn't suffer any for having wrong-sized tomatoes.

Sauro and his people pass through the room then, handing out dishes of the stuff, and everyone eats up. During a quiet spot, I call up Peter's partner, Damien, and Amy gets some snaps of us for both of their phones. And a few on her own phone, too. Soon they'll both be Internet famous.

And we're done, then. I walk Peter back to his table, then mingle with the rest of the crowd, chatting and patting shoulders and shaking hands and giving words of encouragement . . . and handing out order forms for *Chopco* knives.

That's how this all started. A shitty part-time job trying to sell knives, one of a string that I was doing to keep a roof over my head and food in my belly.

Now it's my only job. And thanks to the miracle of the Internet and bored Millennials, it's the best job I could hope for. I work twice a week. I'm not rich, but I have enough money so that I don't have to worry about the rent. Eight thousand people watch this show. And enough of them order *Chopco* knives with my dealer's code that my monthly paychecks are bigger than all of my old part-time jobs combined.

By the end of it, all my clothes are soaked through with sweat, even in the air conditioning, and the guests are filing out happy. Sauro's made fifteen hundred dollars in an hour, and Amy's slumped into her chair, fanning herself with her menu. Her curly brown hair bounces with each puff of air, and I pull a chair over to her and take a seat myself.

"I don't know how you do it," she mumbles.

"I have the easy part! I don't know how *you* do it," I say, waving around at the laptop and webcams wired up to half the outlets and devices in the place, the folders and handouts and dishes which had been full of pre-prepared stages of the dish in various forms of assembly, and pretty much everything that was required to make Jenny's Chopping Spree an Internet sensation. "I'm no good at *this*."

I'm not lying. I would literally take my knives to the studio audience if I had to do half the things she does. I'm just not built for it.

This is why my heart stutters a bit when she says, "I don't know how much longer I can keep doing it, Jenn."

That's not her usual self-doubt or pessimist talk. That's her *I'm being deadly serious Jenn* tone.

"What's wrong?" I ask.

She holds up her phone. It's running an app I haven't seen before. There are a bunch of zeroes behind it. "You broke twenty thousand today."

"We broke twenty thousand, Amy. We broke it. Together! You an' me! Jenn, Amy!" I squeeze her shoulder as I chant the old singsong chant.

That makes her smile a bit. But the smile fades. "You're outgrowing me, Jenn. We're getting too big."

"No such thing!"

"No, look . . . the logistics are getting too big for me. We need . . . we need corporate."

"Amy . . . no. No. Corporate means suits and meetings and desks and big fat guys calling us stuff like little ladies and throwing us into glass ceilings and all that. Corporate *screwed* you, Amy. Remember?"

She takes off her glasses, and her eyes get misty.

Is she going to cry? I hope not. I can't tell. Even with my friends, even with people I've known for years, I can still never tell. It's hard, very hard for me to read other people's emotions. It's why I built the me I did. The manic cheerful girl, the smiling and happiness, the endless energy . . . it works well, most of the time. If I make a mistake, nobody ever blames *me* for it.

"*Chopco* wants to talk sponsorship," Amy says. "Official sponsorship. I'd still be running the show, but I'd have people. And I'd have a boss . . . sort of. I mean, you're my boss. But I'd have another boss."

"I'm your friend, not your boss, Amy." But I'm thinking while she's asking this. "Would this make you happy?"

"It's not about me being happy. It's about making the show the best it can be and getting you the audience you deserve!"

I blink. She's raised her voice, and Amy usually doesn't do this sort of thing.

But then, this isn't the first time she's talked to me about getting help from *Chopco.*

I don't know if I want to work with people who aren't Amy. But . . . I think I'm going to lose her if I don't.

"Okay. Let's do it." I put on my biggest smile, and she puts her glasses back on, lashes fluttering in surprise like her eyes are escaping moths.

"Just like that?"

"Just like that," I confirm. "I improv all the time. So how is this any different? A new recipe, new people in the mix."

She snorts. "You make it sound like we're going to eat them."

I laugh, long and loud, and maybe longer than the poor joke deserves. "Oh! Speaking of that, I got a new chili mix I want to try out. Are you free Tuesday?"

That'll be a little long for the meat, but if it's chili, it won't matter as much. Still not ideal, but I know that Amy works for the next two days, and I don't want to have a feast without her.

Amy wavers a bit, but she nods and offers me a shy smile. I hug her. I need Amy. I don't know what I'd do without her!

No, that's a lie. I know what I'd do without her. It would not end well.

She promises to talk with some people, and I smile and nod and agree to everything she says. Then I collect my jacket and head home. Sauro and his people will help her clean up, and if I touched her computer stuff, she'd get upset.

Once I'm back home, I check *Facebook* . . . and what I find surprises the hell out of me.

They've found *him.* Already.

I turn on the television and put *her* in front of it. "See what you did?" I ask her. But she doesn't reply. She never does.

Then I go and add the wedding ring to the others. Fourteen rings sway on strings hanging from the little sculpture in the closet. And here's sweet number fifteen, silver and shining.

"Don't worry," I whisper to the ring, as I close the door. "He wasn't any good for you, but he'll be good for something on Tuesday."

CHAPTER TWO

The Machine waited, watching the *PowerPoint* slides clip by as the presenter pointed out the salient facts.

He knew all the issues at hand already, but he let the speaker rattle on. The delivery was rough, and the presenter, a small man with a bit of a stutter, clearly needed the practice. The presenter needed it fast, as a matter of fact, since the company's main salesman was gone now.

So The Machine steepled his fingers, ignoring the looks that the two other people in the room kept shooting him as the speaker went on and on.

And at precisely the forty-fifth minute, The Machine interrupted. "Allow me to sum up. Your head of sales has cleaned out every corporate account he can reach and has departed for a long vacation somewhere else while leaving no forwarding address. The triumphant launch of your new product line, which you have gone into copious amounts of debt to expand and develop, now stands at risk of stalling before it's started, unless you manage to obtain roughly half a million dollars before the end of August. Have I missed any salient points?"

He examined his nails while he spoke. Some of his words could be construed as blame, and negative emotions would only hinder his efficient resolution of this situation.

Emotions were the bane of his existence. The world would be so very much simpler if it weren't so emotional and messy. But since humans were unreliable at best, his work was necessary and unending.

Of course, this isn't my real work, he thought.

The gears ground within him, but he held them back, held them with an effort of will as their cold logic built up in whispers against the back of his mind.

There was one step yet to do to arrange the perfect solution, and it required his clients to buy in and cooperate. Without it, the second part of his work would be wasted, and The Machine *abhorred* waste.

"No, no, that's everything," the marketing director said. "We need a lot of money fast because of what Hernan did."

Hernan . . . ah. The name of the former head of sales. The Machine was bad with names. He thought of people as their positions. Names didn't matter so much in his line of work. Names were fleeting, not worth remembering. Inefficient. "And since your head of sales hit the payroll accounts first, the only employees you can call upon for help are within this room. Minus myself, of course. Haha."

"Haha," the company's web designer echoed. There was no real humor in any of the *ha's*. There wasn't meant to be.

The Machine nodded. "Fortunately, your brand has a good reputation and a solid following. Thus a solution presents itself, one uniquely suited to your specialties and expertise."

"*Que* . . . what?" The presenter pulled out a chair and collapsed into it, fanning himself with his folder of notes. It was hot in São Paulo, a muggy heat that opening the windows did nothing to soothe. The fact that the company's air conditioning bill had gone unpaid thanks to recent embezzlement didn't ease matters.

But The Machine was used to the heat, and he spared the presenter a kind nod. "You are now the acting head of sales. We have a marketing director as well, and the head of web design." He put on the smile that he believed came across as fatherly. "Let me tell you of the modern miracle that is called crowdfunding."

Five minutes passed, and they listened, rapt. Five more

minutes passed, and they fired off questions that he fielded with smooth grace. Four more minutes passed, with them mostly talking among themselves and figuring out ways to synchronize their efforts.

And ten seconds before the end of the hour, The Machine stood and snapped his briefcase closed. "This meeting is adjourned. I look forward to seeing your initial efforts in the morning."

They stayed at the table as he left, talking and energized from a new shred of hope. The Machine rode an elevator down to the parking garage, then departed in his rented *Lexus*.

The gears under the hood did their work, and the gears in The Machine's head turned, running over the tasks ahead of him, running over them with eagerness.

One small fix and the world would run smoother. One small fix and a collapsing system would stabilize. The lives of three people would return to normal, and their interactions with their families and loved ones would be less stressful. And then, if their wisdom matched their enthusiasm, the broken pieces of the careers of those harmed by a single act of wasteful greed would slowly be mended as the workers cheated of their fair wages were paid and rehired.

The Machine pulled into the parking lot of the train station and reviewed the algorithm that he'd made for each city. *São Paulo. The locker I want will be number 35.*

It was, and the package was there, as it should be. Good. He had six fallback plans in case it had been missing, but they would have set his timetable back a minimum of fourteen minutes. And the gears in his mind were turning too quickly for that. This would be *perfect*. Having to compensate for such a minor annoyance would be far, far too painful at this point.

Then it was back to the *Lexus*, taking the optimal route, hitting every traffic light at precisely the optimal point of efficiency. It was the late part of the evening for Brazil's work-day, roughly eight o'clock at night. He drove out of the city, to his rented condo, and took the package into the workroom.

There he opened it, and the Machine's breath whistled between his teeth as he beheld the pocket watches inside—three of them, identical, fat brass disks full of springs and gears and time itself. Emblems of order, of perfection, and they were all intact, every last one of them. They'd come through the international parcel post without any damage.

Four years they'd waited there in that locker for him. Four full years since he'd set the machine that was his true self in motion.

Smiling, he put on his gloves, took up screwdriver and pliers, and started his work.

And when he was done, thirty-nine minutes later, he held up the cloth wrap that was now threaded through with gears and springs and the internal workings of the watches. It went over his face, tying in the back with three simple knots that his fingers had practiced time and again. The goggles went on over the holes in the wrap, and he adjusted it so they lined up.

Then he shrugged out of his suit and stood naked as he examined his body carefully. No hair. Not the slightest bit to hold any incriminating evidence or leave behind as a DNA trace.

Only then did he put his tools aside and pick up the paired knives as he descended into the basement. He stepped off the stairs, and his feet sank into the layers of plastic tarps he'd put down earlier in the week.

The man was there as The Machine had left him, bound, gagged, and chained to a radiator. He screamed through the gag as he saw The Machine.

The Machine knelt next to him and flicked out a knife. The man's head jerked back in surprise, and the gag fell from his open mouth, cut neatly through. The Machine noted that he

16

hadn't nicked the man's skin and felt satisfaction. Precision was an important part of efficiency.

"Solingen steel," he explained, his voice calm and monotone. It often was, when the gears were in full turn. "The best in Europe. Perhaps in the world. These are high-quality knives, and they have a single job, after which they will quite likely never be used again. That job is you. You should be flattered." He drew forth the second knife.

"Please! Senhor, please! I have money, so much money!"

"And where did that money get you? It brought you here." The Machine lowered his gaze, trying to calculate the optimal angle so that the man would see himself reflected in the lenses.

"I will give it to you! I will give you every bit of it and more! Please, just let me go!"

"Your attempt to flee was clumsy and lacked forethought," The Machine said. "They would have tracked you down eventually. But I found you first. And now we shall find your money together." He rasped the knife blades against each other, and the man screamed.

"Do not be alarmed. I am going to help you find that element of chaos that made you steal and disrupt your corporation. I will cut away everything that is not wrong, sorting it carefully, and seeking the parts that failed. Everything will be placed in proper order, by the time I am finished. This process is fatal. However . . ."

"Yes? However what? However what? Please!"

"However, if you tell me the account numbers and give me the passwords to access the money, I will end your life before I begin your sorting."

The man cried and begged, but The Machine had heard it all before. The gears in his mind were louder than this failed man's words. His actions had spoken far louder than anything he could say now.

He was faulty.

The Machine would fix him.

Eventually, the man told The Machine the information. The Machine went upstairs, got on his laptop, and checked the accounts. The money was all there, plus a little more. The accounts got drained and moved to a few *burner* accounts that The Machine had set up just for this purpose. In the morning they would be transferred again, to about a hundred different fictional identities that The Machine had crafted a few years ago, back when it was clear that crowdfunding was no longer a fad but a business strategy.

Then he went downstairs again and kept his promise to the man.

It took three hours before he was done. Three hours, and the feeling of the gears clicking into place was a humming in his brain, a tone of perfection that synchronized with the knowledge he was making the world a better place. He was making it *work*.

Finally, everything was sorted, and The Machine got to work cleaning it all up.

Once the tarps were sorted, and every part was wrapped up in taped packages set in alphabetical order, he stepped into the standing shower in the basement and washed away the blood. Only when he was certain that his body was clean did the mask come off, turned inside out to make sure that no hairs remained in the cloth and rinsed. The mask and both knives went into the pile of tarps.

The gloves came off then, cleaned in the steam, and hung to dry. The Machine dressed unhurriedly, donning new gloves, disposable rubber ones to prevent fingerprints. Then up went the processed product, package by package into the trunk of the other car in his driveway.

Six hours of sleep, no more and no less. Then he was back

up, changing into casual clothes. A t-shirt and shorts, indistinguishable from any other tourist.

He left the *Lexus* where it was in the pre-morning shadows and took the cheap, battered *Chevy* instead. This one wasn't rented. This one had been quietly stolen, and the plates swapped out yesterday morning.

The ordered and sorted packages went into a burned-out building in one of the worst parts of the city. It took three triply reinforced garbage bags to get them all in, garbage bags of a type matching the other dumped bags in the shell of what had once been an apartment complex.

The car was gone, stolen by the time he got outside, and he nodded in satisfaction. He had been planning to dump it later, but this was more efficient. The universe approved of what he'd done.

It was too early for anyone to be contemplating violence against him, and his walk was purposeful and confident as he left the slums behind and got to a place where he could call for a ride. A taxi returned him to his condo, where he changed into a fresh business suit and took the *Lexus* to meet his clients.

Their cars were all in the garage when he pulled in, and he nodded in satisfaction. He even let a smile cross his lips, because that was what people were supposed to do when they were happy.

They were still in their offices, the new head of sales, the marketing director, and the web designer. They were clustered around the web designer's computer, and The Machine knocked on the door frame, watched them startle, then smile and wave him in to show him what they had done.

The Machine looked over their *Kickstarter* campaign, gave compliments on the good parts, recommended solutions for the bad parts, and told them to take another day or two to make sure everything was perfect. "Do not forget the possibility of being overfunded. You need stretch goals."

Two days later, Sapotopia Shoes launched its *Kickstarter* campaign for their new Skyfire sandals.

In an unprecedented display of enthusiasm for shoes that had never been witnessed on the platform before, over a hundred different people pledged their money to make the shoes a reality over the course of the first day.

Most of these people were the false accounts that The Machine had set up for just this purpose. Most, but not all. The three remaining staff had done a good job with the *Kickstarter* pitch. And they hadn't been exaggerating the customer loyalty and goodwill that they'd gathered over the years of their existence. Not enough for their purposes by themselves, but once they saw the false accounts throwing their money into the *Kickstarter*, the backers jumped in with enthusiasm.

"The people who run this crowdfunding platform are always on the lookout for fast-growing campaigns," he explained to the marketing director as she gleefully put the finishing touches on her latest ad. "In a day or two, perhaps less, they'll boost your campaign to the top. Your audience on this app will go from hundreds to thousands to tens of thousands. Your job now is to hit the markets that are outside of that reach and bring them together with the new blood."

Two hours later he sat beside the acting head of sales as he made phone call after phone call, telling the various holders of Sapotopia's debt about the *Kickstarter*, and reassuring them that the money would be there if they just did their part. "They'll have to wait a month before the payment arrives, of course," The Machine reminded him. "But they've already sunk money into this project up to this point, so a happy mutual outcome means you don't have to push too hard. A slightly smaller share of a good amount of profit is better than one hundred percent of nothing at all."

And at the end of the day, he stood and paced next to the

groggy web director, mustering his patience as she asked questions that she'd asked three or four times before. The woman clearly hadn't rested, and so he reminded himself that a worn-down gear couldn't handle as much stress. "Get some sleep," he cut her off the fourth time she asked him if he liked the half-a-million-dollar goal update she had planned. "You're going to either go home and rest, or you're going to fold up under your desk and sleep. You're no good to Sapotopia exhausted."

The next morning, before he went into work, he checked the campaign from his laptop. The zeroes next to the campaign's pledge total told him all he needed to know, and the gears in his mind turned again.

He called Randall. "It's done. They don't need me anymore."

"I saw the *Kickstarter*. Kind of unorthodox, but color me impressed."

"They needed a hail Maureen," The Machine said.

"Hail Mary. Hail *Mary*, Curt."

"My mistake," The Machine said, annoyed both at being corrected and at hearing his fake name. Curtis. It was the one his parents had given him, but it wasn't *him*, hadn't been him for a long while.

"No big deal."

But it was. A tiny bit of sand in the gears, a small stutter in the order of things. His memory had betrayed him, even on an insignificant detail.

The joy he'd been riding from his setting things right waned, just a little. "Either way, I'm done here," he told Randall.

"Want me to make the usual arrangements? Are you sure you don't want to stick around for another day or two? The emails I've been getting from the clients are glowing. They'd love to keep you around for a bit longer, pick your brain on other things."

"No. That's not the arrangement."

A long sigh. "I know. Heh. Would it change your mind if I told you the web admin was quietly trying to feel me out to see if you were single?"

The Machine stared at the wall. *Not this again.*

He understood his face and form were considered attractive. More to the point, he presented himself with self-confidence, which was a further component of attraction. And there was his wealth to be considered, as well. Though he doubted the web administrator knew just how well-off he was, he did not think it would hurt her view of him.

Not that it mattered.

He couldn't be The Machine and love a woman. His work, his *real* work came first, and there was no way to conceal it from any woman he might find attractive.

In the space of a few heartbeats, the gears went into overdrive, and he considered excuse after excuse . . . but this was Randall, and that narrowed the list down considerably. Randall was smart and knew a lot about his life already. He couldn't risk a minor lie to Randall, on the off chance it might be caught later.

A snap, as one of the gears fell silent. His euphoria over his work faded even more. He had an image to maintain, particularly among those he had to deal with on a recurring basis. He needed to seem as ordinary as possible, and ordinary men in his demographic were supposed to be seeking out mates.

"I've actually got a few hits on my dating profile," The Machine told Randall. "I was going to use the flight back to do some sorting."

"If you're sure. Miss Blanco is right there and very, *very* grateful after you saved her career."

Blanco . . . The Machine tried to remember the name and failed. It was probably the web administrator, though. "No, I need to get back. I've had enough of Brazil, I think. What's the next project?"

"Well, I've got a couple. Got one near home, actually."

"Cincinnati?"

"Close enough. Columbus. *Chopco* knives wants you to go there and figure out how to boost a cooking webstream they're sponsoring."

"They don't have anyone in-company who can handle this?" The Machine frowned.

"They do, but he's busy with their recent efforts in southeast Asia. And it's a bit too technical and . . . cutting edge for the company. Ha!"

"Haha." The Machine chuckled. He was proud of that chuckle. He spent an hour every night practicing it in the mirror, along with other emotional outbursts.

"Anyway, they think it's got the potential to go from regional to national. We're looking at a mostly marketing job here, and some light financial work. Reorganization of income streams and all that. Seems up your alley."

"Send it to me to review on the flight," The Machine said.

"You sure you'll have time? What with all that *Tinder*-sorting and all?"

It took a second for The Machine to place the name. He made a note to update the app. "I'll make time," he said. "You know I work fast."

"Hopefully, for all those lucky hotties, you don't *always* work fast. But that's your business, man. I'll send you the file."

The Machine didn't get the joke until two hours later when he was in the airport, touching up his dating profile on *Tinder*. It was simply cover, though it had led to a few enjoyable one-night stands, which he terminated ruthlessly after their completion. He could neither enjoy nor risk a long-term relationship.

The simple fact was that he was a serial killer.

He had no plans to change that. It was his place, his purpose in the world, and nothing would change that.

Long-term relationships endangered his work.

And so, no relationship he entered into could last.

Even if he learned to fake empathy long enough to support a mate's needs for the rest of his life, even if he controlled his reactions to the point where he could pass as normal twenty-four hours and seven days a week, the increased scrutiny was a risk he could not afford.

With a nudge, he widened his search area and put his updated profile out on the dating app. The algorithms on this one were simple. With this minimal action, he would be exposed to scrutiny by thousands of women. Statistically speaking, he would gain some hits and could sort through them. If Randall, for some reason, bothered to check, then he would find that The Machine was telling the truth.

That done, The Machine settled back in his seat and waited for the file.

He hoped it would come quickly. Already, the gears were slowing, falling silent. Already the hum of a job well done was fading. The imperfect world was returning, and The Machine knew that soon he would need to fix it again.

CHAPTER THREE

The alarm goes off.

My fist comes down.

The alarm goes across the room, and I tuck the sheets closer around me.

Time passes. I think. It's hard to tell, and I'm dreaming of John Oliver as a puppet telling me my hair looks great.

The phone goes off.

My fist comes down.

The phone hits the floor and keeps ringing.

I tuck the sheets closer around me.

It doesn't help.

With a heavy sigh, I rise and search for my still ringing phone.

I drop down on my knees and sort through the piles of clothes, following the ring as best I can until I dig the phone out. It pauses for a second, and I wonder if I missed it, wonder if all that was for nothing, and I'll have to listen to a voice mail telling me about my car's warranty.

But no, it's Amy. And she's smart enough to ring me until I answer.

"Amy!" I say. "You woke me up. Do you know how" — I was going to ask her how early it is, but I finally manage to focus on the clock — "how late it is?" I say, lamely. I hadn't planned to sleep *this* late. Why was I up so late last night? There was Internet — I remember that. I think it was cat pictures. Definitely looking at stuff online. Was there porn? There might have been porn. It's been a long time since there was anything *but* porn in my life. A throb down below my stomach tells me that no, it wasn't porn, and I'm overdue for some porn or porn-like substitute.

And oh yeah, Amy's been talking through all of this, and I haven't been listening. "I'm sorry, what was that?"

"Jenn, I need you to focus. *Chopco* finally got its stuff in order. We're going to meet my new boss tomorrow. *Tomorrow.*"

"Oh, okay. Have fun with that, let me know how—"

"I need you there!" Amy shrieks.

"Oh! Oh. *Oh* . . ." I understand now.

Amy is smart. Amy is wonderful. Amy is a hard worker.

Amy is terrified of attention.

Put her alone in a room with a stranger, and she'd probably bash down the door to get out—even if the door was unlocked, to begin with.

Me, I'm bad at Amy's stuff. But I'm good with people. They buy the act. They think I'm normal. Well, for long enough, anyway.

"You want me there," I tell her.

"Yes! Uh, yes. Yes, please. It . . . you need to talk to him, too—it's your show."

"Our show. *Our* show, Amy."

"You know what I mean."

"Okay, I'll do it."

"Thank you! Thank you, thank you, thank you, thank you," she gasps. "Okay. Okay, it's at eight tomorrow at *The Guild House*. I'll call you tomorrow to remind you. Bye!"

"Oh, you don't have to call me—wait, eight PM? Not eight AM, right?" The dial tone is my only answer.

She meant eight in the evening, right? Right?

I somehow have the feeling that she did not, in fact, mean eight in the evening, and I'm going to have to haul my sleepy ass up out of bed at six or seven to get ready for this.

I told her corporate was bad news!

But it's Amy, and I said I'd be there, so I'll be there.

That leaves sorting out the rest of the day. Gonna need sleep, so I'll need to wear myself out. Which sucks, because I'd planned on a lazy day, staying out of the heat and surfing the net.

Maybe even porning.

Another tingle down below. *Yes, it's about porning time.* Which isn't enough to wear me out by itself, usually, no, I need something else.

I could go to the gym and work out. Then porn. I have a gym membership . . . somewhere. I'm pretty sure I'm still paid up on it.

I could do that.

Or . . .

Still in my jammies, I sit cross-legged on the bed and pull up the dating app on my phone. Plenty of hits! I can get some release here *and* wear myself out! Both problems are gone at once. Multi-tasking!

I scroll through the list of hits and check out the matches and messages. But wow, it's a lean spot. Lots of frat boys. Lots of shifty-eyed guys who look like they've got a prior or three.

Swipe left, swipe left, Oh, he dropped me a text, "Hey, how are you." Gee how original. Swipe *Left.*

Wait, hold on.

What's this guy doing here?

Cute? Check. Business suit but not a cheap one? Check. Perfect smile? Double double double-check.

Does that make it a triple check? Or a triple double-check? I lose focus and go to *Google* to solve the mystery but find no answers.

Eventually, I remember Mister Hotness and return to him.

Curtis Carver. His initials are CC. Like when you copy somebody on an email. I wonder if he's heard that before?

He lives in Cincinnati, but he travels a lot. He might be out of town. But . . . well, who knows. Even if I can't nab him tonight, I might see him later.

The thought occurs to me . . .

The thought occurs to me that he might be too good to be true.

That he might, in fact, be one of those guys on the app who's actually married.

And that makes me throb in a different way. That makes my lips curve up. That brings out my teeth.

Because if he is, oh, if he is some cheater playing the field, then *she'll* get to play.

And that's as good as — no, that's *better* than a fun night of loving. It lasts longer. It makes me happy.

So, it's a win win win here, any way it works out. Triple win! And no, I'm not going to google that to see if it's a thing. Already did that, and the results were . . . inconclusive!

I swipe right and . . . hey! We match!

Not a surprise, not really. If he ended up on mine, I ended up on his. I get the details and set things in motion. This'll make things easier.

I shoot hotness an *Instagram*.

Hi there!

And oh my god, he responds. Instantly.

Hello. Have we met?

Nope. You wanna?

Do I want to? That's a loaded question.

You put a profile out on a dating app, so I hope you do

Right, sorry. Still a bit jetlagged.

Where are you at?

My home. Until tomorrow, I've got a new project to work on. But it's not far.

Great! Want to do dinner tonight?

There's a long pause, and I hum while I wait. I could get up and fix breakfast . . . well, lunch at this point, but why bother?

My stomach reminds me of why I should bother.

28

Fine, fine. I get up and fix brunch. I sneak a peek at the special packages while I do so, poke them through the foil. Still pretty firm. They should be good tomorrow.

I might be able to do dinner tonight. The response reads on my phone when I look down at it.

Cool. Wanna walk around Cincinnati first? I've got the day free. I type one-handed, while I'm pulling out kale and bacon and artisanal bread.

You move quickly.

Yup. Hope you don't mind. I've rarely met anyone who did. And it's a good way to find the cheaters. They usually can't do a spontaneous day without wifey finding out. They quibble and equivocate and makeup excuses. His next response will tell me whether I get him, or *she* does.

I have a better idea. Your profile says you're in Columbus. My new project is there tomorrow. Perhaps a restaurant tonight? I hear that The Guild House is good.

Well, that's a coincidence and a half! If it is one. He could be trying to arrange something far from home so his wife doesn't catch him . . . maybe. Cincy's a big city, though. It would be easy enough to go somewhere she wouldn't be. No, maybe he's being honest.

I'm game, but let's not do The Guild House. Ever been to Schmidt's? I make the sandwich as I wait for the response and start nomming my way through it.

I can't say that I have. What's a Schmidt's?

I send him a link to the page, and he's silent for a while. *Sure. Seven o'clock?*

Seven's not bad. Seven gives plenty of time for fooling around afterward or for finding something else to do if the date goes bad. This guy is a professional, I can tell.

There's a reason he's not married. There's got to be one. Hopefully, I can scratch my itches before it comes up.

I finish my sandwich and flop back into bed, wondering if I should get another nap before the big date. It's tempting . . .

but my hair's a mess, I'm not sure what clothes are clean and which are dirty, and my car needs gas. None of these things by themselves are enough to be a major thing, but after so many years on this Earth, I know myself by now. There's always something to distract, there's always something to do, and even if I start with only three things, I'll find more things to do along the way.

This is a very fortunate decision because it turns out none of the dating clothes I've dubbed my battle array are clean.

And in the basement where the laundry machines are, I run into Becky. Becky is big. Becky is loud. Becky's whole body shakes when she laughs. She laughs a lot because she doesn't know how to stop talking except when she's laughing.

She's also decided that I'm her best friend ever and likes talking to me.

I put up with it because Becky is an oblivious and useful cover. She has no idea my other half exists. This is why, when the conversation rolls around to *her*, I have to fight to keep from smiling.

" . . . found this guy like just north of here! Chopped all to *bits*. Butchered, was what the news said. That's why they call him Slaughterhouse, y'know?"

"Yeah, I know," I whisper, trying to hide a smile. They still think Slaughterhouse is a man.

"It's just *horrible,* isn't it? Like oh my gawd!"

"Ohmigod, Becky," I agree with her. "Your laundry's done."

She ignores me and keeps on going. "Like who the hell would even do that? That guy had a wife and kids! Now, what are they gonna do?"

They're better off without a husband or father who goes trawling night clubs looking for fast action that's half his age. I keep the thought to myself and make the appropriate sympathetic noises.

"The scary thing about this guy? Nobody knows what

happens to the bits he takes! They think he *eats* them!"

I perk up. "Oh, that reminds me! I'm making chili the day after tomorrow, would you like to come over? You can bring Wayne, if you like!"

She squeals with joy and promises she'll be over.

Becky is one of those women who has a shelf full of cook-books and has never read a single one of them. Becky has never watched my livestream, ever. I'm not sure she knows what livestreams are. I've made Amy promise never to say anything about them to her. It's funnier for me that way.

At the end of it all, I figure Becky adds an extra hour to laundry time.

Then I pop out for gas. It's super steamy and hot today, and the humidity makes me feel like I'm chewing soup when I breathe. And while I'm putting gas in my tank, I remember that I'm out of dishwasher soap, so I run over to the *Kroger's* for more. Then I remember a few more things I'm out of, and halfway through the checkout line, I remember I need more chili powder for tomorrow, and about an hour or two later, I'm home, staring at the clock and looking at myself in the mirror.

My hair, which was a disaster zone, is now a superfund project. My hair needs caution tape and biohazard symbols to give proper warning to all who approach.

I do not have nearly enough time to fix this. But I do have time to mitigate things if I act without hesitation.

"No fear!" I breathe, and strip, eyeing the array of bottles on my shower shelves. "Witness me!" I scream as I turn the water on full blast and charge into the walk-in shower.

CHAPTER FOUR

The Machine left his house at precisely three o'clock, after checking the best routes and making sure there were no accidents or excessive construction delays. There would be construction delays. August was the optimal roadwork season for the region. But thanks to his array of applications and knowledge of the area, he was able to keep his travel time optimal.

After neatly navigating the traffic in his *Camaro*, he waited until he was on the outskirts of the city before he phoned ahead to the hotel, ensuring his room was in order. It was, and the front desk clerk seemed excited to hear he would be staying. The Machine nodded in satisfaction. He'd cultivated a good reputation with this chain.

He had spent seven minutes last night considering whether or not to rent someplace private, in case he needed to disassemble someone, but decided against it. This latest project was a livestream, a cooking show, and The Machine doubted that would require such drastic adjustment.

A stop to his hotel room, and he put himself in order as well. A quick shower and change of clothes would ensure optimal appearance to his algorithmically assigned partner. After that he added a fresh application of cologne. Though it wouldn't last long in the heat and humidity of August, he wouldn't need to maintain a pleasant scent for long. Just enough to ensure that his *date* went the usual way and ended with The Machine sleeping alone in his quiet hotel room.

Up to that point, things had worked perfectly. The gears in

his head hummed and did their work, and he enjoyed the feeling of rightness.

But it did not last.

The trouble started when The Machine crossed the highway into the quaint historical district that housed the restaurant his date had chosen.

The *Camaro* shook, and The Machine's eyes grew wide as vibrations and entirely unexpected sensations rocked his vehicle. He slowed, pulled over, trying to figure out what was happening.

It's the road. The road wasn't asphalt here. The road was made of *bricks*.

Instantly calculations ran through his mind. He checked his GPS app with his phone, calculated the remaining distance to his destination, and compared it to the wear and tear that would be inflicted upon his tires. And the shocks. And the frame. With horror, he realized that this would likely affect his next maintenance window by a factor of one to seven days.

"Hey!" A voice jarred The Machine out of his calculations. He rolled the window down and stared at an irate man carrying bags of groceries.

"You can't park here!" the pedestrian proclaimed and pointed to a sign that sure enough, indicated that parking in this particular location was forbidden.

Horror coursed through The Machine.

He had broken *the rules*.

"Sorry, sorry, I'm sorry," he said, putting the car in gear. "I'll just . . . be off."

The grocery carrying man glared, and The Machine saw him squinting in his rear-view mirror, probably trying to memorize the license plate.

Gears in his mind stopped turning. Now a cold unease filled The Machine. This wasn't right. He shouldn't have come here.

He felt trapped, there in the narrow streets that were paradoxically lined with cars to the point it was barely navigable. Everywhere there were signs telling people where they couldn't park, and that mollified him a bit, up until the point that he realized that several people had parked in places with signs—breaking the rules.

Inefficient. Inefficient! He should have known. This area was historical. It couldn't be changed, couldn't be modernized beyond a certain point.

A breath, two more, The Machine banished his unease. He was still on time, and he took comfort in that. He had arranged to arrive ten minutes early to the restaurant. The brief delay had only been a few minutes. He was still well within the margin of error.

The parking lot was full.

The Machine stared at the signs, and for a second, for a brief second, he considered turning around and leaving.

But no, if he did that, then he would have put himself through this . . . irritation . . . for nothing.

He needed to keep his cover solid, needed to keep Randall unsuspecting.

"A better world," he muttered. "Making a better world. Making the world work."

The next parking lot over was full, too.

With the sun dipping lower in the sky, he was forced to circle and look for a spot. In the back of his mind, the seconds ticked away.

He was late.

He was three minutes late by the time he finally found a spot four blocks away.

The brick streets were like a brick oven, the heat pulling the sweat from him as he power-walked to *Schmidt's Sausage Haus*. He could smell himself under the cologne, and it made his lips pull back against his skull with anger.

This was not how The Machine worked. This was *sloppy.*

This was *unprofessional.*

The sweet release of air conditioning soothed him somewhat as he filed into the old building. Though it looked as historical as the rest of the place, it had at least a few concessions to modern amenities.

The Machine glanced around the place, saw no sign of his date, and winced as he pulled up *Instagram* on his phone. He had already apologized once today, and the prospect of doing so again was humiliating. But it *was* his fault. He had not properly prepared for the weight of history—inefficient, brick-lined, parking-deprived history.

I ran a bit late. Have they seated you yet?

Gritting his teeth, he waited for her reply.

Oh, hey, me, too! I should be there in ten, go ahead and get a table.

The Machine blinked.

Then he checked his smartwatch.

It was six past seven.

She had been six minutes late, and she hadn't sent a message?

The Machine felt the gears slow, and he let out a small breath of air.

Then he got into the line next to a showcase full of obscenely large cream puffs and other pastries and asked for a table for two.

They had a sausage buffet because, of course, they did. The Machine shook his head and perused the menu while he waited.

And waited.

And waited.

Schmidt's had good reviews for its food quality, so The Machine had not eaten prior to his trip north. And now he was stuck in the restaurant, with heavenly savory odors wafting through and into his nose with every breath.

He was hungry. But it was . . . it would be impolite to order before his date arrived. That was what lesser men did. That was disorderly.

But his gaze kept straying to the small buffet, and the metal tubs full of sauerkraut and pepper-stuffed sausages.

Normally he wasn't much for cabbage.

However, his mood *was* getting more sour with every minute that passed.

The Machine had been paid very, very well for every working hour of his time, and after he'd figured life out, several of the idle hours as well. He had built his wealth by continual progress and demanding his due on every rung of the ladder.

And now this woman, this *date* who wasn't even a real date, this aggressive woman who was merely a cover so that the world would not find out the truth about him, was standing him up?

This.

Was.

Intolerable.

He checked his smartwatch again—forty minutes past the hour. He checked his phone again—no new messages.

The Machine was a patient thing, but there were limits. He pulled out his wallet, took out a few bills—

"Oh, wow, cash! Been a while since I've seen that used," a voice chirped in his ear.

The Machine's eyes went wide. His fingers spasmed as he groped toward the knife on the table, that mockery of a blade but still better than nothing . . . and then he caught himself, his wallet hitting the ground with a puff of cards.

How had someone snuck up on him? How?

"Oh shoot, let me . . . whoa, that's a lot of plastic. Sorry, sorry. You're Curtis, right? God, this is embarrassing."

He turned his head and stared straight into a poof of multi-colored hair. It was like one of those mixed cotton candy bags that his parents had tried to bribe him with at the cheap carnivals they loved dragging him to decades ago. Green and yellow and red and *Clorox* blue, and the swirling colors made him gasp in horror.

There was no order to it at all.

The woman knelt down without shame or seeming care for how it looked. Her head was very near his lap as she rummaged on the ground, and there were a couple of chuckles from nearby tables, most likely at the suggestive posture.

The Machine was in hell. This was hell, and she was a demon. That was the only explanation for it.

And then her words sank in. *You're Curtis, right?*

"You're . . . Jennifer . . ." he said, dazed.

This was worse than his worst-case scenario. This was order undone, and another gear ceased its motion, his mind slowing and dulling.

"Yeah!" She grinned and tossed his wallet back onto the table, then stood up with the contents in her hands. "I think I got it all. Sorry again. I just . . . it's been a day, you know?"

"On that, we agree," The Machine managed to grind out. How? How had she managed to sneak up on him? His chair was facing the entrance, and the tables over that way had mostly cleared out. There were archways to the side to the other seating areas, true . . .

That must have been how she did it, he realized. She came in at the exact moment that he was looking at the buffet bar, headed to the other side of the restaurant looking for him, then doubled back from the archway behind him. Obviously.

Still, something in his mind questioned that. It had been years since anyone had managed to sneak up on him. Let alone someone whose hair was . . . was . . .

"Oh, uh, you like?" She grinned at him as she caught him looking and slid into the seat opposite. "It was sort of an accident. See, I tripped while I was run—on my way into the shower. And guess what happened?"

"You were assaulted by a mob of horrific circus clowns that came up out of your drain."

She laughed, throwing her head back and bellowing laughter, which made him wince and regret opening his mouth. Her hair was loud, her voice was loud, and her clothes . . . okay, her clothes were actually tasteful — simple, a white jacket with a black blouse and skirt with pantyhose.

"My eyes are up here."

"So's your hair," he said, not sure if that churning in his stomach was hunger or nausea. It *hurt* to look at that explosion of color.

"Right! My hair. So, I uh, hit the wall of my shower, and I keep all my hair dyes on a suction cup shelf on the wall. And I hit it so hard that guess where it all fell? Yeah."

He dragged his gaze away from that rainbow explosion and caught her gaze, and what he saw there unsettled him.

The Machine was used to seeing desire in women's eyes. He was attractive — he knew that. And he did not lack for self-confidence. But this . . .

This was something he couldn't put his finger on. It wasn't a desire he'd seen before.

This woman is deceiving me.

Well.

He had allocated one hour for the date. And it was almost up. Normally he liked to give each of his *dates* an hour and control the scenario, but her tardiness had just scotched any sense of control.

So he didn't bother with his normal social niceties. Didn't bother with the mask of courtesy that made people more pliable.

"Are you lying about your hair?" he asked, and his voice was cold even to his own ears. "Is any part of that true?"

She smiled.

The Machine froze.

"Every bit," she said and fanned his wallet cards like playing cards. "I think I got all of them. Wanna check?"

He took them, and her hand gripped his, small and hotter than expected. The contact was strange and unexpected, and The Machine's free hand curled around that useless table knife. She was touching him! That was out of the question!

Instinctively he tried to jerk away and felt his eyes widen as he couldn't. He couldn't! She had bizarre strength in those arms, a grip to match his own, and that shocked him almost as much as her stealthy approach had.

"I'm sorry," she said, but her eyes told a different story as she stared into his own, bold and unafraid. She leaned in, put her face close to his ear, her breath hotter than her hand. "I know I've made a mess of things . . . What do you say we skip dinner?" Her voice was low and husky now. "What if I . . . make it up to you?"

The Machine knew this dance as well. But he was a thing of society and conformity, and society, at this juncture, had little use for aggressive women.

But . . . somehow . . . for some reason, as she stared into his eyes with that emotion he couldn't decipher, he felt the warmth rise in his face and in his manhood.

He was hard, and he could not say why.

The Machine took a ragged breath and inhaled the clashing scents of a dozen hair dyes.

That broke the spell, and though he still felt his blood pulse through every appendage, though he strained against his pants, he was more certain of what she was doing.

"And again, you are lying to me," he said.

The Machine slammed the knife into the table, and the woman — Jennifer — jumped in her seat.

For a second, her eyes went wide. For a second, the mask slipped, and he saw the odd look in her eyes replaced by fear. Fear that swiftly turned to anger.

Her grip loosened, and in that split-second, he reclaimed his hand. Scooping his wallet's contents back into his pocket, he stood and left without another word. Only when he got outside did he realize the dinner knife was still in his hand, the blade bent and useless now, and he growled and threw the damned thing away.

Back in his hotel room, The Machine tore his jacket off, heavy with the scent of sausage and hair dye, and threw it across the room. Then he went and washed his hands six, seven, eight times over until the skin was raw. He only stopped when he knew that continuing would draw blood, and he couldn't afford that. He had a job to do tomorrow.

With that, he sighed, then went and picked up the coat. His cards fell out of his pocket then, and he sorted them back into his wallet.

But there was one space open. One slot empty and leftover. The Machine groaned and felt the gears in his mind stop, gone entirely. He racked his memory, trying to figure out what the missing card had been but failed. His normally neat and tidy memory was a wreck, his world shaken by that horrid encounter, and that . . . that *creature* in a woman's shell.

Chaos.

Utter chaos.

The Machine took another breath.

"Work," he said, muttering to himself. "I need to work. Got to find my balance. Have to put things right."

He took a second to compose himself, then called Randall.

The man picked up on the third ring. "Curt? What's wrong?"

"Nothing! Nothing," The Machine said, forcing his voice to obey his will. "I think I'm going to get a head start on the job. Can you send me the details?"

"I can. I mean . . . normally you want them first thing in the morning. But I have it ready right here. Is something wrong?"

The best deceptions had a hint of truth in them. "I had a date. It went poorly."

"Oh. *Oh.* What was wrong with this one?"

"Do you want the list of problems alphabetically or chronologically?"

"So you're sleeping alone, huh?"

Gladly! "Sadly," The Machine lied. "She was less of a hot mess and more of an atomic meltdown."

"Don't stick it in the crazy. Got it."

The Machine coughed.

"Ah, right, vulgarity. Sorry, chief. Let me make it up to you with . . . there's the files!"

"Thank you," The Machine told him, then cut the call and pulled up his webmail browser. Thirteen seconds later, he opened the file and skimmed the contents, taking the details in a page at a time.

Twenty seconds later, he felt his empty belly churn, as a familiar face grinned back at him from the screen.

"No," he whispered, as the world swam around him. "*No!*" he bellowed so loudly that someone thumped on his ceiling from the room above.

"No!" he roared as he stared at the smiling face of Jennifer Doolittle.

CHAPTER FIVE

The alarm goes off.

My fist comes down.

There is no alarm clock there, only the dresser, and my hand smacks the wood stupidly hard.

"Ow!" I yell and sit bolt upright in bed.

"Nope! You don't get to sleep in!" Amy says.

I throw a pillow at her, and she squeaks as it smacks her in the face.

Then I blink, blearily, in the pre-dawn light. "Amy? Why are you in my bedroom?"

"Because I *know* you, Jenn. And because you gave me that key."

"I gave you a key?"

"Back when . . . you know. Steve."

"Steve!" I remember Steve! Steve was her stalky ex-boyfriend. Steve used to leave her threatening messages on her phone. I gave Amy my spare key so she had a place to hide that he couldn't get to.

And then I introduced Steve to *her*. Steve made a pretty good casserole, and I made sure Amy got some. It made her sick, though, so I had to throw the rest of Steve out. I think he was on some drugs or something that tainted his flesh. Such a waste, he had some good muscles on him.

And I'd never taken the key back.

"Uh," I say, as worry begins to stir in the back of my skull. "How often have you been in here since Steve?"

"Oh!" It's dim in the room, but I can see her mousy eyes go

wide under her glasses. "No, I haven't . . . well, I mean you've invited me over, but, I mean, never when you weren't here."

Okay. Okay, now I feel better. Every time I've had her over, I've had eyes on her, and she's never had the opportunity to look in the closet.

I'm not sure what I'd do if Amy looked in the closet and saw *her*.

Except . . .

She's got her back to the closet. Literally in the chair right in front of it.

"Jenn? Earth to Jenn?"

"Uh?" I gather the sheets around me and sit up. "Why . . . you're here. Now. What's the problem?"

"The problem is that you have an eight AM appointment. *We* have an eight AM appointment."

"Oh." I blink. The alarm is still going. What did I set it to last night? "What time is it?"

"Six."

"Great! Wake me up in an hour."

I flop back into the bed and close my eyes.

But the alarm is still blaring. "Hey, can you get that?" I ask Amy.

The alarm gets louder. "No! Get up!" Amy shouts.

She's trying to be forceful. It'd be really cute if I weren't dog-tired. "I had a bad night. Let me sleep!" I moan.

"No! You'll be late!"

I pry my eyes open again. The she-devil is turning up my radio.

"Amy," I say, resisting every urge to hurt her, resisting harder than she'll ever know, "We have two hours until I have to be there. I've *got this*."

"And I know *you*," Amy said. And then she does the unthinkable and turns my bedroom lights on. "And you'll sleep in, then get distracted, and *oh my god, what happened to your hair!*"

"Long story." I scowl, feeling rage flash through me. The memory of that *man's* cold, uncaring face. "I don't want to get into it."

"Okay. Then let's get you into some clean clothes. Ah . . ." She looks around at the heaps and piles on the floor. "Not these."

"They're clean. Mostly," I argue.

"Right." Amy gives me that squint, and then, to my absolute horror, she reaches for the handle of the closet.

"No!" I yell. "No." I repeat more quietly, and I'm out of bed before I know it.

"Uh . . ." Amy stares at me. She has a spooked look in her eyes. I don't like it.

Amy must never meet *her*. And *she* is on full display in there right now. Not hidden.

Distraction! I need a distraction. "I just . . . maybe I need to talk about it. I had a date . . . kind of. It went bad."

"Oh, Jenn, I'm so sorry. He didn't, uh . . . did he t-t-try to . . ."

Amy's been hurt before. It's one of the reasons I keep her near me, so I can make sure she doesn't get hurt again. "No," I say, growling the word. "He walked out of dinner. I broke all my hair dyes washing my hair, and the guy looked at me like I was a freak. Who *does* that?"

Her hand's away from the closet now. "Oh, Jenn. I'm sorry."

I hug her, and she wrinkles her nose. "You smell like sausage."

"Well, I wasn't gonna let dinner go to waste, even if he was a jerk. The sausage was good, at least." I sighed. "Not the kind of sausage I wanted. He was cute. Like . . . grrrr. Just a horrible person on the inside."

"Let's get you a shower, at least." She makes a motion

toward the closet.

"No! No." I grab her hand. "I mean, I want a . . . ah . . . a bath. Yes. I need. A bath. Can you start one going for me?"

"Um, I mean—" She looks at my hand, fast around her wrist.

"Oh, right! Hahahahhahahaha . . ." As laughs go, I don't think it's very convincing. I let her go. "You go get that started, and I'll pick out some clothes."

"Clean ones."

"Clean clothes!" I say, grinning widely. I'm sure I have some around here. Somewhere. Reasonably clean. I did laundry yesterday! Wait, was the basket all underclothes? *Shit.*

But once she's gone and I hear the water going, I open the closet.

Sure enough, *she's* there right in plain view, looking at me from her hook. The layered leather of her face smiles at me through stitched lips, and her eye sockets are empty and black.

But she's there, behind the blackness. I see her smiling back at me, still sated from the last judgment. From the last time we let ourselves go. I'm never alone because she's there with me always, even when her face is hidden away in the darkness.

Next to her, the ring tree stands, and with a sigh, I hide both face and tree behind some winter coats. Then I dig out something businessy. The slacks are leopard print and old, the blouse is golden and shiny, and it really, really doesn't work well together, but that's okay. This is business, not pleasure.

"Not a failed date," I grumble.

That *man* is still on my mind, and I don't know why. He was a jerk!

And yet, those eyes of his had something in them. And I still remember the touch of his hand against mine.

It felt good.

Why?

"Jenn!" Amy yells. "Did you go back to bed? It's seven-twenty!"

"Nooooooo . . ." I try my innocent voice and bring the clothes into the bathroom.

Minutes later, soaking in blessed relief, with the hair dye making small rainbows in the water, I'm enjoying life. Amy is just outside the door, and I'm pretty sure she's got a stopwatch because she's calling in to check on me every five. Or so. *It feels* like every minute.

I give up and tell her about my *date*.

And oddly enough, she's not as sympathetic as I expected.

"So, let me get this straight," Amy said. "You left this guy hanging for over half an hour, made him drop his wallet—"

"Boosh! Cards everywhere!" I giggle. "You should have seen his face. It was hilarious."

"Did you tell him that, too?"

"Well, no. I even helped pick them up!" I gave them back, too, all except for one of them. That one wasn't a credit card, though, just an old piece of paper with an address and numbers scrawled on it, so whatever.

"And then you perved on him."

"I got aggressive, that's all," I say, and maybe I'm pouting, but who cares.

Amy cares. "You're totally pouting, aren't you?"

"He liked me being aggressive in the texts! He knew what he was getting into."

"What he wasn't getting into," Amy snarks back at me. "I can't blame the guy. You're kind of the bad guy here, Jenn."

And again, you are lying to me, I hear in that smooth, deep voice.

I growl. "He called me a liar. He can go hang. Whatever. It's done, and I'll never see that asshole again, so good riddance."

She drops it, and I finish up my bath with an hour to spare. Pantyhose, I'm thinking, even though the heat's over ninety today. I won't be outside that long, and the slacks are a little tight after I wedge them over my butt. Been a while since I wore them, and I'm eating a lot better and a lot more regularly these days.

And this reminds me. "Don't forget! Chili tomorrow!" I remind her.

"Yep. And livestream this afternoon, but before any of that, breakfast with the *guy* this morning! In one hour!"

"But I haven't even had coffee," I whine.

"We'll get it on the way. Cup half full so you don't spill it. And carry a change of clothes in case you do."

"Okay, *Mom*."

It's not even *Starbucks* coffee. But I drink it anyway. She's driving, insisting on driving, and that's fine. It's not that far anyway, just down High Street. If it weren't August, we'd walk it, but we have to meet *the guy*, and she doesn't want us sweating too much. That's fine. The drive gives me time to look out the window and watch my city, watch the old buildings with the new storefronts, and stare at the streamers strung across the street. This is the Short North. This is where people come to party, sometimes in some pretty non-standard ways. Some people think it's seedy, but it isn't. It's just used to doing its business behind closed doors and not hurting anyone.

And it has the most awesome pride parades ever! I'm not gay, so I don't march, but I buy rainbow flags and cheer my heart out every June, and I love to see all the people up there having fun and just being themselves.

We have to park a little way down. Even at this hour parking's an issue. Another reason I'm glad to leave the driving to Amy. I pull out my handbag as we get out of the car and hug it tight to remind myself it's there, and I shouldn't forget it. It's leather, leather I tanned myself.

This one's cowhide, mind you.

I can't use the *special* stuff out in public.

The Guild House is all wood and glass and light. Exposed wooden beams, hardwood floors, smoothly varnished counter and tables. Glass chandeliers hang overhead, unneeded in the early morning light.

The color of choice is brown, light brown and dark brown, and I clash awesomely.

"So, where's the guy?" I ask Amy. She's texting.

"Got him," she says and motions toward the side, where there's a slightly rounded room partitioned with glass, a curtain hiding its occupants. Not exactly a corner room, given that there isn't a door in the partition, but close enough.

"Right!" I smile big. "Let's go talk business. Good cop bad cop?"

Amy just glares at me. "This is *important*. This is *Chopco's* chosen contractor! We need him on board!"

I breeze through the room, smiling back at her, feeling on top of the world. "Relax! You can totally be bad co-ooooooooooo . . ."

My voice goes into a drawn-out squeak.

It's him.

There against the back of the room, at the table, staring at me with his face stony and unmoving.

It's my *date*.

I stare at him.

He stares at me, elbows on the table, and hands folded. Mister Burns folded, without the creepy smile.

"I . . ." *Wanted to fuck you, you asshole!* I want to scream. I want to shout. I want to flip the table on him.

Are they nailed down here?

I don't know. And it's that thought alone that stops me

until more cautious thoughts pop into my head.

I can't do that. Can't do any of these things.

This is too important to Amy.

"I . . . need a minute," I tell him, drawing a shuddering breath.

"Of course," he says, nodding, and is he smiling? Oh, is he *smiling*? Because I'm going to lose it if he's smiling, but no, he's not. There's no expression at all on there. His face is concrete, stone, the sidewalk, flat and unmoving.

I burst past Amy, who stares at me as I go, and I ignore her questions and barrel into the restroom. There I jam a fist into my mouth to keep from screaming.

What the hell have I gotten myself into?

CHAPTER SIX

The Machine watched Jennifer Doolittle flee and sat quietly at his table. He didn't drink his carrot juice — freshly juiced — or eat his croissant — freshly baked — because he was working and the meeting was underway.

"Ah . . . oh dear. Sorry," the short, brown-haired woman who followed in her wake said. "I didn't . . . she didn't . . . Jenn is gonna need a minute."

"That is acceptable," The Machine said. "By my watch, we have three before she's late." He smiled in a way that he had spent forty-seven hours in total practicing in front of mirrors over the years. "I have no doubt it will take her longer to compose herself, so we can start off by talking over technical details. You, of course, are Amy Buller, the technical director?"

"I . . ." Her face was red.

"Please, have a seat. Not that one," he told her as she slid out the chair across from him. "You seem confused. Your friend and I met last night, under less fortunate circumstances."

"Oh boy," the technical director said and eased herself into the third chair, the one off to the side. "You're . . . you must have been her date last night? Awk-*ward*."

"I was." The Machine controlled himself. He had spent years learning to keep his emotions from affecting his face, and it paid off now.

"Why . . . I mean, no offense, but it seems like — " She raised her gaze, found the courage to meet his gaze. "Why did you ask her out if we're going to be working together so closely?

50

That doesn't look too good, you have to admit."

And The Machine found himself on the horns of a dilemma.

The date had been a train wreck, a dumpster fire. *Disorderly*. It had been sheer bad luck, the whims of some unseen chaotic force, a glitch in the algorithm of the dating app that he had angrily uninstalled from his phone and downvoted in the wee hours last night.

But the technical director's statement indicated that she thought that he had set the date up deliberately, knowing who Jennifer Doolittle was beforehand.

If he denied that and spoke the truth, then that would be admitting weakness. It would be admitting that he had not researched their portfolio before last night, and that admission would paint him as negligent to anyone who was not familiar with his methods. It would heighten distrust and cause problems with their collaboration.

Moreover, it would be admitting before them that the world still held variables that he could not control, that reality was not ordered, and that there were events in play that made his efforts to organize and improve the functionality of his society and the larger society that was humankind, futile. It would be affirming to himself that he did not have the capability to fix the world.

However . . .

If he lied, if he claimed that the date had been deliberate, then The Machine would appear to be more influential to these clients.

And moreover, it would get his mind off the whims of a fate he neither believed in nor could consider without some degree of fear. The more he dwelled on that, the slower the gears turned.

But the thing that decided him, above all, was the realization that neither this woman or the *other* would have the wherewithal to prove him a liar. He was risking nothing by fabricating a falsehood here.

All these thoughts ran through his mind in a matter of seconds as he stared at the technical director.

"Yes." The Machine nodded, keeping his gaze on the woman's glasses. "I asked her out, so to speak, to take her measure, to gauge her personality and practices before we committed to this joint venture. Had she passed the test I set before her, we would have enjoyed a mutually satisfactory meal and met under better circumstances today. But she did not."

The technical director flinched as if he had threatened to strike her. The Machine considered his responses and chose the one that seemed more comforting. "Please understand that her actions do not reflect upon you. You are here on time, without causing a scene or invading my personal space, as is she. So far." He glanced toward the restrooms, then checked his watch again—one minute to eight.

"She's not—I mean—you can't tell her that!" the technical director said, barely controlling her voice.

The Machine raised an eyebrow. "Can I not? What is stopping me?"

"Because she'll never forgive you if you tell her that! You . . . she told me about the date. She didn't mean any of it, but I felt bad for you! But it turns out you set this up all along! Now I think it's your own fault." She seemed almost surprised at the words coming out of her mouth. "And if I think you're at fault, then she'll never forgive you. She'll . . . she doesn't forgive stuff like that. If she gets hit, she hits back."

The Machine paused.

And while he did, a familiar figure stalked through the archway. The Machine checked his watch.

Exactly eight o'clock.

"Thank you for your punctuality," The Machine said,

gesturing to the chair across from him.

Jennifer Doolittle smiled. Then she slid the chair aside with her foot, pulled another one over to the table, turned it around, and sat. Her legs were apart, straddling the chair, and her arms were crossed over the chair back as she glared over at him. "You're welcome," she said, her smile bright and her teeth clenched.

"Miss Doolittle—"

"Call me Jenn."

"Jennifer—"

"Jennnnn," she said, sounding it out.

For a moment, The Machine debated getting up and walking away again.

But only a moment.

"Jenn," he conceded. And in his mind, he christened her The Diva. It helped soothe the gears a bit. It was a more accurate nickname for her. "It is my hope that we can put personal feelings aside and collaborate to make your livestream the phenomenon that it deserves to be. Please, make no mistake. I want to see you succeed."

"Buttttt . . ." The Diva drawled.

"But what?" he asked, quirking his eyebrow again.

"But there's a catch. There always is. Any time people say that, there's always a *but* attached."

"I assure you I have no but attached," he said. For whatever reason, this made the technical director giggle, then conceal it with a choking noise.

The Diva, though, blinked a few times and studied him without speaking. Confusion in those eyes, confusion and that other thing he'd seen, that thing he couldn't place.

"So you want to see us succeed," The Diva said and drummed her hands on the chair. "Without a but."

"No buts attached," The Machine reassured her.

"We're doing fine so far."

"Yes, you are doing fine. Many would count this as a success. But they would not see it for what it is, and what it is, is an opportunity."

"For what?"

The Machine controlled his reaction to the sloppy grammar. "Right now, it is a success, but this state of affairs is not a permanent one. You need to change, to exploit your current synthesis with the zeitgeist of the general populace, and grow —"

"Please spare me the buzzwords," The Diva said. "We don't do corporate. This is a friendly local show, and we're doing just fine without stuffy suits and boardrooms and slogans."

"Some of that is correct." The Machine nodded. "However, the key statement is wrong. You *were* a local show. You are more than that now. And I do not think you realize just how much you have achieved, and how very small a window you have to exploit this."

"Okay. What do you think we're missing?" The Diva asked.

The Machine smiled. "I've observed two episodes of your show and checked the statistics against similar productions. From that, I have extrapolated a list of improvements, consolidated them into some simple documents, and readied them for your examination." He offered the thumb drive that was the summary of this morning's work. All in all, it hadn't taken long. Jenny's Chopping Spree was nothing special, and the modest improvements he had offered would boost it to *Chopco's* satisfaction. He could finish his business here and be gone, leaving this unstable, aggressive woman to her own devices.

The Diva stared at the small, plastic thumb drive in his hand. She made no move to take it.

The Machine cleared his throat.

"Two episodes?"

"Yes. Number four and number thirty-two."

The Diva turned her head to her friend. "Which ones are those again?"

The Machine stared. "You don't remember your fourth episode?"

The Diva grinned back at him. "No. Why should I? I've done it—it's done. It's past. What's the point in remembering it? I've got the shows recorded so I don't have to."

"You started this livecast in March. It's been less than a year."

The Diva's tone grew cool. "Yes. And we've got twenty thousand viewers now. So maybe a little less patronizing and a bit more respectful? Kay? Thanks!"

The Machine opened his mouth, but The Diva had already turned back to her companion. "Seriously, Amy, which ones were those again?"

"Well, four was the one with the Takoyaki. Remember? The one where the octopus was attacking you, and you made all the tentacle porn jokes?"

"Yes, that one," The Machine said, allowing himself a slight frown. "I checked the numbers on your demographics then, and I wasn't surprised to find that your older viewers disliked that one, due to the inappropriate nature—"

"Eh, fuck 'em. Old people clutch their pearls all the time. Our biggest viewer bloc is eighteen to thirty, right, Amy?"

"Thirty-two, but yes."

"Right, episode thirty-two! That was the other one." The Diva snapped her fingers.

"No, I mean age thirty-two . . . oh, whatever," the technical director said and fiddled with her phone. "Here we go! This one is where you were making circus food and deep-frying candy bars. The one with the grease fire."

"Oh yeah! I was wearing a burn mask for the next few

shows, and people thought I was really burned." The Diva laughed. "I was, but it didn't show as badly as we were pretending!"

"Wait," The Machine said. "You actually got burned from that stunt?"

"Stunt?" The Diva stared at him, honest puzzlement in those piercing eyes. "That wasn't a stunt—that was faulty equipment."

"To be fair, you kept yelling you were gonna kick it up a notch and pushing the temperature up," the technical director said. "Even though I kept telling you it was copyrighted."

"Psh, like Emeril Lagasse is watching my show."

"He might! Or worse, his lawyers might!" The technical director turned her face to The Machine. "I had to beep her voice out every time she used those words. It sounds like she's swearing now!"

"I was swearing after the grease hit me!"

"Yeah, I had to beep those, too. Jenn, just take the thumb drive, *please*."

"Fine, fine."

But her hand closed on empty air as The Machine withdrew it.

"You nearly burned yourself to death on your livestream, and then you shrugged, stuck a bandage on your face, and continued cooking? That wasn't planned? There were no safety measures on hand?"

"No. It wouldn't have happened if I'd known it was going to happen."

The Machine tried to untangle the nonsensical sentence. It hurt, and a gear ground and slowed. "The octopus, though?" he said, a note of desperation creeping into his voice. "That was planned, at least? You didn't really have an octopus trying to eat your face?"

"I certainly did! It took a lot of work to keep that little

bastard from sucking out my eyeballs! Look, are you going to give me that thumb drive or not?"

The Machine snapped it in half.

The two women fell silent, staring at the remnants and plastic shards in his hands, then back up to his face. Then down again, then up again.

"Is this a joke?" The Diva asked. "I can't tell."

"No. It's wasted work." The Machine shook the shards onto his napkin and rubbed his face. "Does something go wrong with every episode?"

"Well . . . no, not really," The Diva said, her eyes shifting back and forth. "There was that one where we set off the fire alarm."

"And the one where that goat got loose, and you had to chase him out of the kitchen," the technical director volunteered.

"And when I used the wrong-sized lid for the mixer, and tomato goop got all over me," The Diva said, reflectively.

"*And* the one in the abandoned factory where the squatters shot at us," the technical director recalled.

"Okay, no, *that* one worked out fine. They were nice after I offered them some of that shovel cake!"

"You beat that guy half to death with the shovel!"

"Well, he shouldn't have shot at me then!"

The Machine stared at The Diva, feeling disbelief rise up from deep inside. "Someone shot at you."

"Yeah, we were doing old-style depression-era hoecake. So we went to a place that had burn barrels and tried to bake some, and this crazy squatter thought we were burying a body!" The Diva laughed. "It's fine, though. We worked it out."

"You didn't call the police?"

"No. He was cool. And he thought the shovel cake tasted good. Can't call it hoecake anymore, though, since y'know, it sounds kind of like an insult now. And shovels are a lot easier to find than hoes anyway."

"We don't have accidents or dangerous things happen every episode," the technical director protested. "Our last show went off without trouble."

"That would be number forty-two?" The Machine asked.

"Yep! I think." The Diva looked to the technical director again, who nodded.

"The reason I broke the thumb drive," The Machine clarified, "was because the recommendations I had for you weren't based on an accurate analysis. I thought your show was something that it was not."

The Diva considered his words. Then she got up, turned the chair around to the normal way, and sat down. His gaze traced her form as she did so, and he wasn't quite sure why. But something about the gold of her blouse drew his gaze.

"Hey. My eyes are up here," she whispered.

He found them again, and the gears in his mind jumped into overdrive.

That knowing smile . . . she thought he was still interested in her!

The Machine reached for the right words to say and couldn't find them.

She leaped into the silence. "So you did all that without knowing what you were getting into, huh? Well, there's a simple fix!"

"I'm listening."

"Come watch us do the show!"

Some vestige of caution, some random instinct of self-preservation flared up and told him *no*. Warned him that this way lay madness.

But The Machine had long ago learned to transcend his petty instincts, had forged himself into a creature of reason and logic.

"Very well," he agreed. "I shall do that, and we shall see what you have to show me."

CHAPTER SEVEN

We talk details through the rest of the meeting and get some breakfast to go. I manage to get through it without punching Curtis. It's work.

It helped that he broke the thumb drive.

Up until then, I thought he was a stuffed suit. But now? Now he's actually got something of a backbone in there. Now I think there's something to him.

And I totally caught him checking out the goods earlier. He's playing it cool since I called him on it, but he is interested.

But oh, he is *not* off the hook.

And the fact that I have to work with this guy? It itches. It seriously chafes!

I chow down on a *pain au chocolate* in the shelter of Amy's car. The pastry is pretty much a chocolate scone with delusions of grandeur, and it's flaky, and bits go everywhere.

I expect her to chew me out for making a mess, but she's quiet as we drive back to my place. I sneak a few glances, and her focus is on the road—good, responsible Amy—but her thoughts seem to be a million miles away.

"So," I say.

"So."

"So-so?" I ask.

"Definitely a so and so," Amy says, but now there's a hint of a smile on her lips.

"Solo or no go?" I ask.

"Okay, what?"

"Do we need this guy? Do we *really* need this guy? Because I'm not getting a happy, and if you're not getting a happy, then we can walk away. Just . . . ghost him."

She glances at me, then back to the road. Morning traffic is bad, but we don't have far to go. Lots of stops. "You sure this isn't personal, Jenn?"

"What? No! Why would it be personal!"

"You just smashed your biscuit thingy."

I look down at the shards of pastry on the floor and chocolate stains on my fingers. Shrugging, I start licking my hand clean. "Mffkay, maybe itffs a libble pfersonal," I admit.

Amy laughs. "No, no, seriously, we need this guy. It isn't just him. It's *Chopco*. He's the one they chose for this, and if we get him on our side, we can get things like an advertising budget and bigger sponsorships."

"But we're doing fine!" I protest.

"Yeah, but we could be doing *better*. And, Jenn . . . I want people."

"I want people, too, but sometimes you want things you can't have," I lie. I get most things I want. It just takes some work and a little imagination sometimes.

"Yeah, you wanted him, and now it's weird."

I mime a gun going off under my chin and flop dead.

"You smeared chocolate on your neck," Amy tells me.

"Bah. Probably shouldn't have used the licked fingers," I agree and mop my chin with my sleeve.

"But no, seriously, if we want to make the show better, we're going to need a crew. I can work a laptop, and edit footage, and set up a few cameras, but I'm not the best at it, and hiring people who are better will take money."

"We have money!"

"We have enough for your rent and our supplies and a few nice things, but that's about it. And the laptop I'm using is from the Bush administration."

"It still works . . ."

"That thing is so old it thinks *JavaScript* is what baristas do to your coffee when you ask for latte art."

"Ooh, that's a good name for it."

"That's not the name for it at all!" Amy pulls up next to my building.

I pop the door open with my not-sticky hand. "Okay. Okay, I'll give this guy a shot. And if he doesn't work, I'll give him a *shot*." I make the gun fingers again. "Because we'll *fire* him."

She shakes her head and pulls the door shut after I get out. Then she's off again, her little *Kia* tootling down the side street and heading for her place, probably. It's Amy—she probably planned out the route with two or three little stops for errands that she'll finish in an hour or less. She's like the opposite of me.

No.

No, that asshole in the suit is the opposite of me. Amy's likable, and that guy's like a bottle of *Tide*. Pretty on the outside, but toxic on the inside.

But then I remember his fingers snapping that thumb drive—the noise it made as it broke.

There might be something to him. Maybe.

But he also called me a liar, and nobody else ever did *that* before—not even *her* victims.

I get to my building's door and haul out the keycard, and while I do, my phone buzzes. I glance down at a text symbol and click it.

Hey there, Jennifer, it's Chris Devon, remember me?

No.

I drove you home a few nights ago. Been thinking of you ever since.

Oh yeah! Mister Two First Names!

I grin because I'm pretty sure I know what's coming. This is going to go one of two ways, and I'm pretty sure . . . yep, there it is.

Unsolicited.

Dick.

Pic.

I check the windows next to the door.

Is that his SUV down the street? It looks like it. Oooh, a stalker.

I guess an ordinary woman would have been scared. She would have thought this guy was a predator.

And he is.

But I'm different. Sure, he's a predator, but I know a better one.

And this day has me rattled enough that I know she's *hungry*.

I turn slightly toward the car, hold the phone out at length, and just examine it for a while. Let him think I'm interested. Then I drop my key and bend over, giving him a nice view of my ass.

Finally, I type back.

Wow.

Thanks. I've been blessed.

He hasn't—he really hasn't, but that's neither here nor there. I slide the key through the lock and head inside, typing as I go. *Give me a bit. Juggling a few things.*

Take your time.

I get back to my apartment and check the clock on the microwave. Then I look at my refrigerator. There's room. Chris Devon looked like he had a lot of fat on him, so the good parts shouldn't take up *too* much space.

But . . .

Does he deserve it?

Does he deserve *her*?

I think so. I feel so. I feel it in my gut, in the hunger that's rising now, the eagerness to play. I had a good buzz going on from the last guy, but then Mister Curtis goddamn Carver killed it. Buzzkill! He couldn't be more of a buzzkill if he were personally spraying beehives with poison!

I'm getting off track. Eager. Angry. I get on *Facebook* and search for Chris Devon. Yeah, that's him. Friend request!

It's approved, instantly.

What's up, babe? Pops up on messenger.

But I ignore that. I look at his profile.

Oh. Oh, look at that. He's in a relationship.

I check the microwave's clock again. There's just time. *Just.* If I hurry. I tell him.

You've got me hungry.

Hungry for sausage?

No, I had that last night, I think as I open the closet, and pull *her* out. In my bag she goes, along with *Chopco's* latest assortment, and a few sex toys on top to hide them. Then a change of clothes over the whole assortment.

Only after that's done do I respond to him. *Very hungry. Are you nearby?*

I can be there in two minutes.

I look at the bag, and I want this, I want this so bad. I'm drooling, swallowing saliva down my throat, but I force my fingers to tap my phone. One last test. One last chance for him to prove he's a person and not meat.

My husband is here. We'll have to go somewhere else.

A half a minute.

Forty seconds pass.

I know just the place.

I smile then.

"Playtime!" I tell her as I scoop up the bag.

Then I jog out, and sure enough, that SUV is Chris's *Ford Explorer*, and I slide in with an eager smile. He grins back, eyes wide and surprised behind his *Ben Franklin* glasses, and he rubs my thigh as he pulls out into traffic.

His hand tries to go higher, but I grab it. "Not yet," I breathe into his ear as I lean in close. I feel him shiver. "This place you have. Private? Nobody knows? Nobody will see us?"

"Yeah," he whispers back.

I rub his wrist, stroking it, pumping it as I lick his ear. It tastes like *Axe* body spray and dead skin, and I hate it, but then I take a bite, and he yells and jumps and nearly plows into a *UPS* truck. Horns blare, and I back off and laugh as he takes the wheel with both hands.

"Ow! Jesus. Is there blood? It feels like there's blood."

"There's blood," I tell him and sweep my tongue across my lips to show him. Spread it around, get rid of his bad taste with salty iron.

"Ah. Yeah. I'm . . . I'm into it. Just . . . nowhere that shows. 'kay?"

"Pinky swear," I lie to him, and I put my bag in my lap. The metal inside clinks and I smile as I imagine what's to come.

It's a small condo off Sawmill Parkway. And it's quiet at noon, and the neighbors are a way off. It has that new housing development smell. "You live here?" I ask, knowing he doesn't. He's *in a relationship*. There's no way he'd take me home.

"Naw, this is a friend's. He travels and shit, so he doesn't mind me using it." He pulls into the driveway and leers at me. I smile back, and once we're inside, he's all over me, hands roaming as his tongue tries to catch mine.

I give back as good as I get, and he breaks free, looks at me with amazement, glasses foggy from my breath. "Shit!"

"No," I tell him sweetly. "Not shit. Fuck! That's what we're here for, right?" I lie.

"The uh, the huh, hah, the bedroom's upstairs," he says, hard and throbbing against me, so hard that I can feel it through his jeans.

"Go ahead," I say, and I put the bag on the counter, pull

out something frilly. "I'll be up as soon as I change."

"Sure! Sure. Yeah, I'm into it!"

He slaps me on the ass as he goes, and I giggle. It sounds fake, but I don't think he notices.

Once he's gone, I shake my head. My heart is pounding—the warmth fills my belly, and I feel looseness between my legs. But it's not from him. Not from *him*, not the way he thinks, and I giggle as I strip naked.

For once, I don't have to worry about plastic tarps! This is somebody's house!

I'm panting, feeling the blood pounding in my veins, feeling my nipples harden in the air conditioning, feeling the tingle across my lower lips as wetness slicks me, and I pull *her* out of the bag. I put her over my head, fumbling until we can both see, until my eyes fill her sockets.

Then I pull out a *Mark Three Chopco Fileting Knife*.

My lips open, and I feel the layers of skin on my face pull back, feel her smile with me.

"Hello, Jenn," she says through me. "Let's play."

I giggle, and this time it isn't fake. We pad up the carpeted stairs, toward the open door above. And just before we reach it, a thought strikes me, and it's too delicious to ignore.

"Hey!" I call out. "Daaaaarrrrrling? Could you humor me? Could you say . . . something like . . . You need to exploit your current synthesis with the zeitgeist of the general populace? And do it in the snottiest, most stuck up voice you can?"

"Uh . . . sure?"

He does.

It's the last thing he says.

After that, there's a lot of screaming and blood, and good ol' Chris Devon's got more fight in him than I anticipated, but it doesn't help him in the end.

I sit there, just sit for a while as the glow fills me, the afterglow better than any sex. I think I might have orgasmed a few times, too. That's a thing that usually only happens when I've been too long between kills, but it's a nice bonus when it shows up. Maybe I should write to Vogue? *Dear Vogue, I have found the secret to better orgasms through ritualistic murder . . .*

Everything is right again.

I did a good thing. Another cheater is dead.

I'm going to feel so good for a long time now. I've got my buzz on.

But eventually, I realize I have to wrap things up here. No matter how good it feels to bask in the afterglow.

I prop Chris's feet up on the pillows as the blood splat splat splats down onto the floor. It's soaked the bedding up around his head, and I need it to all drain in that direction, to bleed out of the meat I'm about to harvest.

I detour to the bathroom and clean up. There are some cuts on my arms from where he dug his nails in, and I treat those with hydrogen peroxide and bandage up. A bruise on my hip is tender, and I can tell it'll blossom plum purple in a day or so. It made walking here a little painful, but it isn't anything major. That's where he got me with his knee. For a guy who drives all day, his legs were pretty strong!

I have to turn the sink's faucet on and off with the palms of my hands. No bloody fingerprints! That's just asking for it. Downstairs I slip on a pair of rubber gloves from my bag and haul the rest of my gear upstairs.

Time's short. I have a show to do later.

So, chop-*chop!*

CHAPTER EIGHT

The first thing The Machine did when he got back to his hotel room was sort through the livecasts. He watched several episodes of Jenny's Chopping Spree.

He had thought they might be kidding, telling him about that shovel cake episode. But no, but no, there it was in glorious shaky-cam, with The Diva running after people off-screen, waving a shovel that dripped molten batter. Then a flash-cut later, there she was with a few grungy-looking squatters, sharing what were essentially cornbread pancakes with them and laughing and talking about the pros and cons of burn barrel ovens.

The episodes they did in the restaurants usually didn't have anything as dramatic. Usually.

But a significant portion of the shows that took place in the field had something unexpected and dramatic happen during their recording.

The conclusion was obvious. The math didn't lie.

To get such a ratio, they had to be staging the incidents.

"So why did they lie to *me*?" The Machine muttered.

It made no sense. He was *Chopco's* duly appointed interface, the middleman who could approve funding and boost their show to the big leagues.

And *Chopco*, he knew, would not mind if certain aspects of the show were staged. They would most likely be happier if it were staged. Less chance of having their star sidelined by a falling frozen turkey, or knifed in a dark alley, or whatever calamity drew itself to Jenn.

The Machine was midway through the next episode before he realized that he had thought of The Diva as Jenn.

He felt his eye twitch.

This was an irritant. There was no need to think of people by their names. They were jobs. They were problems to be fixed, puzzles to put right, and then they were to be discarded. It was pointless to retain names, and the more he used them, the more risk that he'd waste brain cells devoting them to pointless memories.

Names got in the way of the gears. Names made things personal.

Names were a thing from a time before he had become The Machine.

Irritated, he checked his watch and took a breath in surprise.

He was almost *late*.

That was unheard of! Lateness was a character flaw in others! The Machine was *never* late.

There was no time to change, no time to shower, no time to work on an updated document, and no time to buy a new thumb drive, for that matter.

Not that The Machine had anything to put on a thumb drive. No, until he figured out the reason for their deception, he had no constructive feedback to offer.

These thoughts ran through his brain as he grabbed his briefcase, threw his jacket on, and headed out the door at the fastest gait he could manage without appearing unseemly. His footfalls clicked on the tiled floor as he pulled up his phone and checked for messages—nothing.

He tapped the address they had given him into his phone, put it on the dash of his *Camaro*, and headed into traffic.

He drove as quickly as he could without violating traffic laws or taking undue risk, but his gaze kept flicking to the dashboard clock—the merciless countdown.

Up until the traffic accident, he had hope.

But once he saw the lights up ahead and the slowing lines of cars, he felt that hope fade and die.

It was just one accident and not even a serious one. Two cars pulled off the road, dented, with a police car behind them, lights on.

But naturally, *everyone* slowed down to get a look.

The Machine reached for the gears, found them cold in his mind, silent and disapproving.

The last minute faded, and he sobbed. With trembling fingers, he pulled out his phone.

And the next time traffic stopped, he typed in a message he'd never had to send before.

I'm going to be late. Tr

He stopped at the last word. He'd been about to write *Traffic problems*, but that was an excuse. And The Machine never made excuses.

I'm going to be late. I am taking steps to minimize the issue.

There. There, that conveyed contrition without weakness. That seemed safe. He sent the message off and waited in the slow herky-jerky roll of traffic past a spectacle.

His phone buzzed at five past, and The Machine took a deep breath.

Here comes the reckoning.

He had prepared for ire, for mockery, for a petty dig at how the tables had turned.

But what he received instead had him staring, glaring at the phone in his hand as it shook, his fury making his hand tremble.

Take your time. Jenn's running late.

"Why?" he roared.

A horn blared.

He looked up from his phone, swore, and yanked the wheel to the side.

The semi missed him by inches.

The Machine breathed hard and let the phone lie where it had fallen.

And in the silence, Siri told him to turn left onto Trabue Road.

Gritting his teeth, The Machine put his hands on the ten and two spots on the wheel and focused on the drive.

A few minutes later, he was pulling into the back lot of a church. Only one other vehicle was there, a *Kia* sedan that had seen better days. The hatch in back was open, and the technical director looked up from where she was wrestling several boxes out onto the asphalt.

"She won't be long," the technical director reassured him through foggy glasses. Then she squinted. "I don't know if it's a good idea to wear a suit for this."

"I only packed suits for this trip," The Machine said, smoothing his jacket down. The sun was high in the sky now, and it bore down without mercy. He was sweating, but within tolerances. Although it was fairly muggy here. It probably had something to do with that lake he'd passed on the way in.

"Um. Well, maybe you could at least take the jacket off. Just for this."

"Why don't you tell me what this *is*, first?"

A car engine roared, and The Machine flinched as a *Ford Explorer* sped past him, bumped over a parking lot divider, and came to rest between two parking spaces.

"Hey!" The Diva called out through the open window. "Sorry I'm late! I did an errand for a friend, and I didn't have time to return his car."

The Machine checked his watch. Twelve minutes.

"I suppose traffic did not help you much," he said as he regained his composure, showing just a bit of concern, concession. Yes, that was the proper response.

"Nah, traffic was fine." The Diva grinned. "You need any

help there, Amy?"

"Um . . ." Amy gave one more tug, and a frame of canvas and metal pipes clattered out of the back of her *Kia* and hit the ground in a sodden green mess. "Yes. Yes, I do."

"Great!" The Diva flounced over, paused, went back and turned the SUV off, then came back again and started picking up the scattered contraption on the ground.

"What exactly are we doing here?" The Machine asked, after a silent moment.

Whump!

He barely caught the bundle that she tossed straight at his chest. "We're portaging." The Diva grinned. "You know how to row a canoe?"

"What."

Ten minutes later, with his jacket off and the sweat rolling down his face in the glare of the sun, The Machine was rowing a goddamned canoe.

"So basically," The Diva said as she rowed with her oar on the other side, trying to match his painfully uneven strokes, "that's the *Shrum Mound* over there. Big Native American burial mound."

"Adena tribe," the technical director added in, stuck between the two of them and not budging as the collapsible canoe wobbled and bobbed and struggled under their combined weight.

"All right," The Machine said, marshaling his patience. "And I asked what that had to do with *us.*"

"Well, we were going to cook a Native American recipe there! But the trust or whatever that owns the place didn't want us doing that."

"Entirely unreasonable," the technical director added in. "Or maybe they thought it was disrespectful, so that might be fair."

"Then why are we heading there now?" The Machine

asked, grimacing as the canoe tried to pull to the left. Again. He corrected, got it straightened out perfectly . . . but he hadn't accounted for The Diva's frantic corrections, and now they were pulling to the right. "You're trying too hard. Let me even us out," he suggested.

"You don't know what you're doing! You haven't been in a canoe before today," The Diva scolded him. Then to his surprise, she turned them further to the right, paddling with splashing disregard.

The Machine glared back. "I'm the one who doesn't know what he's doing?" he hissed and paddled them straight again . . . then winced as his last stroke was a bit too strong and rocked the boat so hard that for a second he worried about capsizing.

That infuriating woman sent him the sweetest smile as she set them straight with a single stroke. "So anyway. We can't do it on the mound itself, but that island up ahead? Perfect view with the mound as a backdrop." She pointed at a small, scraggly, tree-filled island smack dab in the middle of the lake.

"Wait," The Machine said, staring back and forth from the Mound to the island, now well off to the right. "That is our destination? Not the mound itself?"

"Yyeeeeeppp."

"But we've been paddling toward the Mound for the last five minutes!"

She glared at him. "Yeah, I know. Why do you think I kept trying to turn us right?"

"You. Didn't. Tell. Me. We. Weren't. Going. Over. There."

"I figured you'd just follow my lead. For once in the two days I've known you? You're here to watch us at work, remember?" The Diva sighed and paddled them back toward the island.

After a moment, and a few deep breaths, The Machine put

his paddle back into the water and helped her row. Between them, the technical director sighed with relief.

But a thought struck him as they were pulling the canoe onto the rocky, bramble-filled beach. "The owners of this island, were they more agreeable to filming here?"

"Um," the technical director said and coughed.

"Totally!" The Diva said, as she pulled a *No Trespassing* sign out of the ground and threw it into the lake. "I'm sure they won't care at all."

The gears in The Machine's mind clunked to a standstill.

And then a strange feeling overwhelmed him. As he watched this woman, this chaotic, walking mess flip her multi-colored hair into a ponytail and tie it back, he found himself laughing. Not hysterically, or the practiced, careful *haha* he'd spent years cultivating.

It was a laugh that said for once that he didn't have to worry. For once, he didn't have to be in control of the situation.

Because this was in no way his fault, and no consequences could befall him that he truly had to worry about.

This roaming avatar of chaos was solely responsible for everything, and all he had to do was avoid the inevitable karma and the blast radius when it finally fell upon her head.

In fact, The Machine rather thought that he'd enjoy watching her fall.

His good humor lasted until he finished and saw her smiling at him, beaming, teeth parted, eyes aglow.

And that thing was back in her eyes again, that feeling he couldn't identify.

"There you are!" she said. "I was wondering when you were going to stop taking it so seriously. Thanks for helping get us here, now kick back and watch us go!"

The Machine found a comfy spot on a rotten log and watched them set up. The technical director got to work setting up an old-school camcorder, hooking it up to a laptop.

"Oh!" The Diva bounced over to him.

"Oh?" He asked.

"I meant to give you your card back. The one I grabbed at *Schmidt's* and forgot about."

"My card . . ." The Machine's brain hummed and clicked. He remembered the empty slot in his wallet. "Ah, yes. My card. You took it, then?"

"By accident. You left so fast I didn't have a chance to give it to you." She grinned wide and pulled out a business card.

The Machine took it and found it unfamiliar. "*Chris Devon*," he read. "*Uber's best Goober*?"

"Whoops! Wrong one!" Before he could blink, she tore it from his hands so quickly that he barely saw her move. "Let me see . . ." She rummaged in her handbag. "Huh. Not in here. Now, where did I leave the thing?"

Behind her, the technical director straightened up and glanced back through the trees. "Jenn! We're gonna miss our window!"

The Machine checked his wristwatch. "You already have."

"No, I mean the *real* window."

"Amy . . ." The Diva sighed. "Did you lie to me about the time again?"

"I might have set us to start an hour later than usual today. Maybe."

"Amy!"

"No time. We're on in ten. Nine. Eight . . ."

The Machine watched her dart out of the scene. She strolled back in front of the camera, whipped out a hatchet, and buried it into a tree. "All right!" she screamed. "Who's ready to go *chopping*?"

Then followed a little knifeplay, as she circled the campfire and the portable stove set up on it. The Machine was in her world now, cares gone. He folded his arms and waited, a studio audience of one to The Diva's personal half-hour of culinary cuteness.

"Today it's wild rice soup, Native American style! But we're doing it near a special place . . . the *Shrum Mound*! Amy, get us a shot!"

The Diva flourished the knife and pointed, then made little cuts that suggested she had carved the mound like a pudding. "So that makes this a whole new recipe. I call it Rice with Shrumshrooms!"

And she sliced the mushrooms up, her mouth going all the while, going on through the history of the place and how the Native Americans gathered the ingredients.

It all went smoothly until she tugged on the hatchet on the tree trunk.

It groaned.

It cracked.

The Diva's eyes went wide, and she stopped pulling and started backing away.

And with slow, horrible grace, the tree fell.

The Machine stood and realized that the tree would crush him.

He sidestepped and winced as the bark scraped his nose.

Across the way, The Diva stared at him, hatchet dangling from limp fingers. The Machine watched as she licked her lips, eyes almost crossing as she stared at his wound.

Whump!

The tree was down. It had flattened the log he was sitting on. It would have killed him if he hadn't moved.

"Oh, uh, sorry there. Ope," The Diva said breathlessly.

The Machine shrugged. He put a handkerchief to his nose and pulled it away bloody.

"Here," The Diva said. She stomped through the underbrush and took his shoulder. Her hand was hot through the silk of his shirt, hot as her breath as she stared up at him. She took the handkerchief from his unresisting fingers and dabbed his face.

And for his part, he stared down at her.

That thing in her eyes. That feeling he couldn't place—he knew it now. That feeling was hunger.

It was hard to say how long she dabbed at his face, and after a moment, he put his hand on her shoulder. She made a noise, somewhere between a gasp and a sigh and a squealing chatter.

The Machine paused.

She paused.

The squealing chatter came again.

"Was that you?" The Machine breathed.

"No, I don't know what the hell that is," The Diva whispered back.

"Guys . . ." the technical director broke in.

The two of them looked to her, saw her point, and looked to the shattered tree stump, and the dozen or so raccoons that were skittering out of it, squealing and chattering and charging straight toward the food.

"Oh, hell, no!" The Diva shouted as the little furry bandits got into the rice, two of them biting into the sack and pulling. Grains burst out, showering over the pot as another little trash panda tried to roll the thing off into the bushes. "Get the bastards!" The Diva yelled and charged into their midst, kicking and stomping.

The Machine shook his head.

This was a stunt. This had to be. This . . . chaos couldn't be real.

They have wasted my time.

He reached for his phone and found his pocket empty.

The Machine looked down.

A raccoon chattered at his feet, clutching his phone.

The Machine stared at it.

It hissed and puffed itself up.

"You are making the biggest mistake of your very small

existence," The Machine told him.

The raccoon lunged for him.

Five bloody seconds later, The Machine looked up to find every living thing left on the island staring at him.

The technical director was frozen in horror, the light of the camcorder winking as it broadcast the whole scene to thousands.

The Diva, mouth open and face bloody, was staring at him with some sort of unholy glee filling every bit of her smiling face.

And every raccoon that was still standing was backing away slowly and putting down their stolen knives and spoons and bowls.

One of them chirped and looked toward the bag of mushrooms. It stretched out a paw.

The Machine closed his clasp knife with a *snick*.

Every raccoon turned and bolted for the water, diving in and swimming for all they were worth.

"That. Was. Awesome!" The Diva screamed and hugged The Machine.

It took every inch of The Machine's self-control to refrain from opening the clasp knife and stabbing it into her back.

"Uh," the technical director coughed. "We're going to have to edit most of that . . . out . . ."

"Oh. Right. Okay. Back to the recipe!" The Diva turned to the shambles of the cooking instruments strewn around the island and gathered up what she could. "Well, they scattered and dirtied the first batch, so we're gonna hack the recipe! Now it's raccoon stew with rice and shrumshrooms!"

The Machine stared.

Of course, she's going on with the show.

Dazed, he retrieved his phone and swiped off the twitching, severed raccoon paw. Then he pulled up the livestream.

The numbers were over fifty thousand. In the middle of the day, fifty thousand people tuned in to watch the vermin-slaying bloodbath.

This has to be faked, The Machine thought to himself.

Then he looked down at the bloody handprints on his shirt where The Diva hugged him, drew him close. And he wondered.

But the gears turned. Deleting a raccoon had been nowhere near as satisfying as removing a faulty human. But it was one less overturned trashcan, one fewer attic broken into and destroyed. In a small way, The Machine had saved some part of society a small disruption.

The show finished, and the two women started cleaning up their equipment. He declined a hot bowl of raccoon stew. The Diva didn't seem to mind his lack of appetite, and she happily tucked into her own lunch.

"Hey," she said when she had finished, and he'd helped pack the equipment back into the canoe. "Do you want to have dinner with us tonight? It's chili, and it isn't raccoon."

"I'm not sure I should," The Machine said.

"Consider it my apology for almost killing you with that tree." Her eyes were wide, and she took a few quick breaths, probably lost in the memory.

The Machine stared into her eyes, found the hunger again. *No. Bad idea.*

But the words that came out of his mouth were. "All right, yes."

Why?

She smiled and got back to work, brushed against him, smeared against the blood still drying on his suit, as she helped load up the last of the gear.

This is ludicrous, The Machine thought, as they pulled into the water and rowed with smooth grace, used to each other's rhythm. His frayed nerves calmed as they went, though.

At least the worst is behind us.

Ping!

The Machine looked up in time to see one of the connecting

pins snap and fly out of the canoe.

Ping ping!

Two more went.

The Machine closed his eyes and palmed his face with both hands, as the collapsible canoe lived up to its name.

At least the water was warm.

CHAPTER NINE

"Jenn. You're not listening to me."

"Of course, I'm listening to you!" I tell Amy. She's cute when she's worried. Her face gets that lost look, and she waves her hands around more.

She's wearing her older pair of glasses, the ones with what I call *celibacy frames*.

She's wearing them because her best pair of glasses are at the bottom of a rock quarry lake. Along with her laptop, her camcorder, my phone, and my traveling cooking set.

"You might be listening, but you're not hearing me," Amy says, rubbing her eyes. "Jenn, we're sunk. Without that equipment, I can't edit the recording. It went up to the cloud, so we've still got it, but I can't post it to the usual places. The *Patreon* subscribers are going to be calling for their footage tonight, and it won't be there! I can't compile the highlights or edit out the inappropriate things, so we can't post a *YouTube* version!"

"Amy . . ." I put my hands on her shoulders. "We've got this. We'll work through this. You're still alive. That's the important part."

She looks down, takes a long drink from her mug. We're in my apartment, cleaned up after our dunking, and drinking hot chocolate. I had to drag her here afterward because I was worried about her. I still am.

"I had everything preset," she says, staring into her mug. Like me, she's got a towel wrapped around her hair, spa-style. It took some serious washing to get the stagnant quarry water out of our hair. "That laptop was like an extension of my body."

"Amy, we can get another one. I can buy you one tomorrow. No, tonight. *Micro Center's* open late, right?"

"Jenn . . ." She sighs and pats my hand. "I can get new equipment. But it's going to take time to configure it. I need something specialized for this and for doing business stuff, too. It's going to take me days to get everything straightened out once I've got the hardware. We . . . we might have to cancel *Buca di Beppo's*."

"What? *What*? No, we can't! It took forever to land that agreement!"

Buca di Beppo's is a chain restaurant that makes family-style dinners. I'm supposed to be making lasagna at their Columbus venue on Friday. *This* Friday.

They were a tough sell. It took a whole lot of convincing for them to give us this shot. If we flake, if we break the agreement, then they won't give us another.

"Isn't there anything we can do?" I ask Amy.

"I . . . just let me think. Just let me think, Jenn. Maybe I can figure out something."

I nod, then get into the fridge.

It's been a long day, and we burned a lot of calories. Time to prepare the chili!

I smile as I pull out the paper and plastic-wrapped packages, the cuts I prepared last Friday. Into the grinder they go!

"Hey," I call back to her. "I lost my phone."

"I know. What do you need me to check?"

"Is Curt still coming?"

"This is the third time you asked me to check that."

"Yeah, but he might have canceled."

"Well, he didn't."

"You didn't even check it!"

"Look, he would have called if . . . fine, okay, Jenn."

I hear her rummage and tap her screen. While she does, I start mixing the spices and baking the beans. The sauce is next, and that takes a little more time. Fresh onions to chop for that and my eyes are all leaky as I work. But my hands know the way, and the knives are familiar in my grip. I've worked under worse conditions, and this time, the meat isn't fighting back.

"How are the numbers?" I ask her.

"I don't know. All my metric software is on my laptop."

She sounds so miserable. Poor Amy.

Knocking at the door. "Come in!" I call.

"I'll get it — " Amy starts, but the door opens before she can rise.

"Hello! Hubby's going to be late!" Becky burbles, bustling into the kitchenette. "Oh, that smells delicious!"

I threaten her with a spoon to her throat when she tries to dip a hand into the pot. "Wait! Not done yet."

She freezes.

Her mouth trembles in an *O*.

And I realize that I'm not holding the spoon, I'm holding the knife.

"Oh! Ha, just kidding!" I grin wide and watch Becky's gaze flutter down to the knife and back up to my face. I remove it and put it in the sink. "Sorry, it's been a day. I'm on . . . edge."

I watch good old Beckster's eyes flash through a number of thoughts, and then she brays laughter. I laugh with her, and she wanders into the living room to talk with Amy.

My air conditioning does its best to keep the heat down, but it's August, and I'm in a warm kitchen by the time all is said and done. I'm glad I had a bath beforehand, because woo, I'm sweating!

There's a buzz.

What's this, now? Is someone buzzing from outside the building?

I poke the intercom button. "Y'ello?"

"It's Curt."

"You sure are."

"Haha."

There's a long pause.

"Are you going to let me in?" Curt asks.

"Oh! Was that what you wanted?"

"Yes."

I consider playing dumb some more, but no. He was interesting this afternoon. I should reward that.

"All hail the raccoon slayer!" I say as he knocks on the door. "Enter and receive your reward, oh hunter of bandits!"

But it's not Curt. It's Wayne, Becky's husband, and he looks really confused. He's in a rumpled, sweat-stained suit, and a bulge under one arm where I know he's got his service revolver. "Racoon slayer?"

"Wayne!" Becky squeals. "How was work, bubby baby?"

Wayne holds the door open and grins, and behind him, I see Curt come up the elevator. He looks around, looks at my door, and nods to me. I lift a hand to wave.

"Work's going great, boo!" Wayne calls back. "We'll catch that serial killer for sure this time!"

I see Curt freeze mid-step and wave to him. "Hey, Curt! Come join us!"

Wayne looks around, then holds the door for him, looking him up and down. "Who's this then?"

"Curtis Carver," the man in black says, smoothing his suit. The difference between his clothing and Wayne's is the difference between a sports car and Amy's *Kia*. But Curt has a briefcase, too, so I figure that's like a V-8 engine on top — clear advantage here! The two men shake, and Wayne keeps squinting at him.

"Stop giving him the cop eye and come sit down, bubby!" Becky shrieks.

A flash of irritation crosses Wayne's face. "Yes, dear," he says, testosterone visibly shrinking. To be fair, it's a wonder there's any left after six years of being married to Becky. I like her, but that's because I don't have to live with her.

"Curt's with *Chopco*. And he kills raccoons!" I say as Wayne finds a seat on the couch next to his wife. I stir the chili and ignore Curt's gaze on my back.

"Only when I have to," he clarifies in that smooth, deep voice. "And technically, I'm a consultant for *Chopco*, helping these two enhance their show."

"Gonna try and sell me knives, there, Curt buddy?" Wayne asks.

"No. That's her job." I hear the scraping of one of the kitchenette stools being pulled out. "What's yours?"

Becky interrupts before Wayne can answer. "He's a detective for the CPD! He's in charge of the Slaughterhouse task force!"

"We used to call ourselves the *Slaughterhouse-Five*, but after the last couple of killings, they upped our funding, so there's eight of us now," Wayne says. "Spoiled our joke, more's the pity."

"A Kurt Vonnegut reference? I approve," Curt says.

"What? Who?"

"You said *Slaughterhouse-Five*, did you not?"

"Yes, like the movie. I don't know any vonny gut guy," Wayne replies.

There's a silence. I'm the only one close enough to catch Curt's quiet sigh.

"Anyway, Curt's doing a good job," Amy says, "even if it might not matter now."

"Don't talk like that, Amy! We'll work it out," I say as I drain the fat out of the simmering meat.

"Work what out?" Wayne asks.

"Amy's upset because we had an accident in a canoe, and

lost a lot of our hardware," I cut in.

"A canoe? What were you doing in a canoe? Those things are dangerous!" Becky shrills.

"You need to replace the hardware immediately? You don't have any back-up units?" Curt asks.

"No." I can almost hear Amy's teeth grinding. "And yes, we do need to replace it. But we couldn't afford —"

I hear the sound of plastic hitting the counter — thick plastic.

There's silence. I look over, and the gleaming black credit card on the counter is emblazoned with *Chopco's* logo. Curt stands next to it, hands folded behind his back. "I can authorize up to a twenty-thousand-dollar expenditure at this time. Will this suffice?"

"I uh, wow, I . . ." Amy stutters.

"It's not enough," I say. "She'll have to configure things. She doesn't have all the business doodads and technical settings, and formats and doormats and things."

"I see. How much time will you need to accomplish such a thing?" Curt asks.

Amy chews her lip. "Well, days at least. Which means that we'll have to cancel the *Buca di Beppo* slot."

"Explain." Curt studies her, taking a seat on the barstool and steepling his fingers together. The curve of his jaw draws me, and not for the first time, I want to run my hands along it. I stir the meat into the chili pot instead, then start adding the final ingredients bit by bit.

Amy launches into technobabble, and I tune out, focus on the recipe. This one's turning out *well*.

I knew that the guy had great taste when I found him. Now, what was his name again?

"Charles Forsmythe, the Third," Wayne says.

"Thank you, that was it!" I say, smiling. Then I put my hand over my mouth. Whoops!

"What did you say?" Curt asked.

"Sorry, I was trying to remember an ingredient," I say as I put the lid on the pot and turn back to the group. "What were we talking about?"

Curt has his briefcase open and his jacket off. He's tapping away on a laptop inside the case.

Wayne's leaning forward, with Becky gripping his arm. Amy's up near the archway of the kitchenette, sneaking peeks at Curt's work.

"We were just talking about Wayne's work!" Becky squeals. "And that Slaughterhouse killing last week!"

"I was out of the country then," Curt says, quickly. "So I was unaware of this development."

"Yeah. Lots of clues from Charles's murder. But lots of bad luck, too," Wayne says, leaning forward and steepling his fingers. He looks like he's trying to copy Curt, but he's doing a bad job of it. I giggle, just a bit.

I am so buzzed from Devon, earlier today. And from the fact that Wayne's right in the room with what's left of Charles Forsmythe, *the Third* and doesn't even know it!

"I don't believe in luck," Curt says. "Are your clues insufficient?"

"I didn't believe in luck either," Wayne says, scowling at Curt. "But then I started working these cases. Video cameras in the areas Slaughterhouse visits burn out the day before or have corrupted footage. Witnesses who should have seen everything are out of position or hammered out of their minds on booze or drugs. We've had one guy call in with a suspect description, and what happens? He has a heart attack and dies *while he is on the phone with us*. It's insane. But it happens."

"How long has Slaughterhouse been active?"

"About six years," I say.

I feel Curt's gaze upon me and have to fight not to giggle.

"Close, but not quite," Wayne mansplains. "More like five.

That's the first confirmed killing."

"Well, you'd know." I offer him a tight smile. "Chili's up!"

Amy helps Becky haul out the little table from its nook. I only use it when we have company. Everyone gets a bowl, and I bustle around, putting out saltines, and focaccia bread, and side dishes. Amy helps by pulling out two liters of pop and bottles of a microbrew that I decided to buy on a whim.

"Hey, you got any gluten-free sides?" Becky asks. "I'm trying to cut down on my carbs, watch my weight." She takes a long pull of her *Coca-Cola* throwback, made with pure sugar. It's her third cup tonight.

I smile and pull out some gluten-free rice cakes, along with the remnants of a veggie tray. The tomatoes are a little saggy, but everyone only really eats the carrots and celery anyway, so I figure the odds are good.

"It's only a matter of time, though," Wayne says. "He's accelerating. There was originally a four or five-month period between his kills. Now that period is down to weeks."

It is true.

It just hasn't been as satisfying lately. The buzz doesn't last as long. I feel like I'm going through the motions, and I don't know why.

But I'm feeling good good good from Chris and everything else that happened today, so I don't dwell on it. *Don't be a sad Jenny.* I hear in my mother's voice.

Ah, why am I thinking of her now? Don't wanna spoil the mood.

"I'm sure you'll catch him, or her, in due time," Curt says.

"What? No, Slaughterhouse is a guy," Wayne insists. "There are no female serial killers."

"History would seem to disagree with you," Curt offers.

"I mean . . . women aren't serial killers anymore, anyway. Women are too busy with being offended on social media nowadays," Wayne laughs a bit. Nobody else does. He clears his throat, looks annoyed, then digs back into his chili.

"This is great stuff!" Becky bubbles into the silence. "How do you do it? I've never tasted anything like this?"

"Sorry, it's a secret recipe." I grin.

"Come on, you can trust me!"

I cannot, in fact, trust Becky. Not with this or anything else. Becky cannot be trusted.

I don't even hate her for it. She's a platonic solid of Becky. It's actually kind of comforting to have that one acquaintance who thinks she's everybody's friend who isn't friend quality to anyone.

But it's Amy who saves me the trouble of finding an answer. "Forget it. I've told her she could make millions if she sold the recipe, but she won't budge."

I spread my hands. "Sorry! It's . . . ah, I have to keep at least one secret I don't stream. It keeps me sane."

I'm not lying.

If I didn't do what I did, I'd lose it completely.

And *she'd* never talk to me again.

Wayne takes a third bowl. Amy and Becky make do with two apiece. But Curt only takes one, and he's still got half of it to go while the others are on their seconds. He's distracted, tapping at his laptop while chatting with Amy.

I'm tempted to butt in, but for once I don't feel like it. Being bold with Curt got me ditched in a restaurant. Something about him is throwing me out of my comfort zone.

Why?

For a moment, I flash to how he took down that raccoon, how he caught twenty, thirty pounds of fur and claws and muscle in midair and gutted it like a fish.

For a second, I feel that warmth south of my belly again.

I didn't expect a prissy businessman, an office drone city-slicker to handle that the way he did.

There're hidden depths to Curtis Carver.

Wayne's phone goes off, and we all stare at him. "Detective Button," he says, standing and heading toward the back of the apartment. He doesn't make it, as whoever's on the other end babbles, and his face brightens. "Really? Sawmill Parkway? This is great news!"

More babbling.

"No, no, no, I didn't mean it like that. Poor guy. An *Uber* driver? Well, could have been worse, you know. At least this one isn't a *third.*"

I stifle a giggle. I know what *this* is about!

"They found *what*?" Wayne says. "Now that's a clue! All right, I'm on my way." He ends the call and turns to us, face glowing. "Slaughterhouse just struck again! Not even a week later! This could be our big break!"

"Oh, *honey!*" Becky shrills. "You go get 'em!"

Wayne's already out the door.

I look at Becky. She looks back, eyes wide. "Poor guy! Think I can get some of that pot for him? He'll be working late on this one, and he'd really appreciate a bite to eat tomorrow!"

Yeah, and anything I give you is gonna end up in your guts, Becky. But I grin and fill up an empty *Cool Whip* container for her. Poor folks *Tupperware* is what momma called it!

Wow, that's the second time tonight. Why am I thinking of her?

Silence in my apartment now. Amy and Curl are deep in discussion. Finally, Becky coughs. "I guess I'd better turn in. Thanks for dinner!"

"No problem!" I grin, my teeth stained with Charles Forsmythe, the Third. She happily takes her food and departs.

I drift over to the counter. "So what are you two techies tech-talking about?"

Amy's face glows at me. "The fact that we won't have to cancel *Buca's* after all!"

"See! I told you not to worry! I knew you'd figure it out!"

Amy glares at me. "We're not canceling because Curt is loaning us his laptop. Which has almost everything I need set up on it."

"I'm giving it to you," Curt says, typing fussily. I watch his fingers stroke the keys with easy grace. He's good with his hands.

"Mm?" I blinked. Amy said something and I didn't hear it. "Sorry I missed that. What was it?"

Amy rolled her eyes. "I said, we're only pulling this off because he just came through for us. Big-time. Not because of luck or anything like that. People had to move their butts to make this happen!"

"Which is how the universe works," Curt tells me, and I frown at him. He continues, seeming not to care about my glare. "Nothing significant happens unless people make it happen. And in this case, though indirectly, you made it happen."

"Oh?" I ask. "Did I wave a magic wand or something?"

He shakes his head, taps a few keys, then turns the laptop around to me.

I look at the numbers on it and blink. "That's got to be a mistake."

"It isn't."

According to the web page he's showing us, three hundred thousand people have watched our livecast.

I mean, it's more than that, but my eyes focus on the three hundred and some in front.

"How?"

"I'm still reconstructing it," Curt says. "But as far as I can tell, *PETA* filed a formal statement calling the video raccoon snuff porn and attempted to remove it from your stream provider."

"They *did* get it removed," Amy says. "But not until after enough people had seen and pirated it. Then they started posting it up all over the place. Which made *PETA* freak out more and tried to censor it."

"Which initiated a chain reaction, from your viewers who either dislike *PETA*, or dislike authority, or both." Curt continues. "The end result — this show has gone viral."

"Back episodes are getting new viewers doing an archive crawl," Amy says, her eyes moist. "It's a chain reaction, Jenn!"

"Hence the card." He points to that big lump of heavy plastic on the counter. "And my willingness to gift you my property."

"I . . . wow." I sit on the barstool next to him. "I don't know what to say."

So, I lean in and kiss him instead.

I see his eyes open wide, and his hands clamp on my shoulders. I half think he's going to push me off, but his lips are hot against mine, his breath pouring into my mouth.

His grip eases.

There's something in his eyes. I don't know what it is. Something deep, something cold, but he's warm — his breath is warm, and I feel his tongue flicking against mine, and moan as I ease into his arms. I'm on fire, and throbbing heat pounds my groin, and I feel him relax . . . then stiffen, as he pulls himself back, pushes me off. But gently.

"Miss Doolittle," he says, and his voice is husky. Whatever was in his eyes is gone now, and only confusion remains.

I make a noise that's two-parts want and one-part question.

"I'm not going to go into the reasons that was inappropriate. Please do not do that again."

Now the noise I make is one part want and two parts disappointment.

And my gaze flicks downward, to his tailored, bespoke slacks.

He may be saying one thing, but oh, that bulge is saying another.

"I'll, uh, I'll see myself out. Thanks for dinner. Goodbye, guys!" Amy says, all in a rush, packing up the laptop in a hurry.

"I'll be leaving as well. Good *night*, Miss Doolittle," Curt says, fixing me with a steady stare.

And two minutes later I'm sitting by myself, among the dishes and detritus.

But I'm smiling.

"He wants me," I say to the pot full of all that remains of Charles Forsmythe, the Third. "He just doesn't know it yet."

CHAPTER TEN

The Machine wanted her and he knew it—knew it and hated himself for it.

It made no sense.

He found himself remembering, replaying her embrace repeatedly in the back of his mind. Three times he had to restart the shipping order. Three times, he almost sent his backup laptop to Zimbabwe, because his mind wandered while tapping in the information on his—thankfully waterproofed—phone.

He had always considered himself an asexual being, a thing beyond petty lusts and desires. Such things were inefficient. Such things impeded his work, impeded the gears.

The gears in his head were silent, while his hormones raged. He could feel their disapproval—feel them looming cold and sullen in that quiet place that he had built to stand against a world that cried out for balance.

Why do I want her?

Focus.

He needed focus.

The Machine sat down and started typing up a report to *Chopco*.

After a while, he rose and headed downstairs for breakfast.

The hotel was primed for the business class traveler—as such, it didn't bother with free breakfasts, things called *continental* that consisted of gummy eggs and ancient communal waffle makers, bacon pre-crisped and more prone to jab a gum than provide any useful nourishment. No, it had a simple cafe with the expectation that all receipts would be charged back to corporate headquarters, for accounting and tax deduction purposes.

The report went no more smoothly than his order.

At least the croissants were good. Though not as good as the chili that Jennifer had —

The Diva. Not *Jennifer*. The Diva.

Black coffee washed the taste from his mouth, wash her face from his mind.

And then a message popped up on his phone.

He hesitated, dreaded to answer it. Thought of Jenn — of The Diva's face again, and popped the message open.

It was the technical director, and though some part of him was disappointed, the overwhelming emotion was relief.

The Machine was too unsettled to speak to The Diva right now. There was too much risk there, too much chance of saying something . . . unplanned.

Hey, it's Amy. Thanks again for the loan!

I told you, it's a gift. Keep it.

Right, okay. I also wanted to apologize for Jenn. I think she made it weird.

She did. But that's all right. I will simply control my contact with her from this point on.

Are you sure it's okay? I mean, if someone did that to me, some guy kissed me out of the blue, and I didn't want it, then I wouldn't feel okay.

The Machine tried to remember her name, failed. He took a minute, pulled up one of the livecasts, and checked the credits before returning to respond.

Miss Buller, I can assure you that I am a professional. I have been paid, and very well, to perform a job here. You need not worry about me. I shall see my task through.

Okay. I wanted to make sure no bridges had been burnt here.

The Machine deliberated on the next question. But after a time, he decided it was worth asking.

She doesn't plan any of this, does she?

Do you mean the show? She pitches ideas at me, and I work out the details. So she plans that.

No. I mean the tree, the raccoons, the canoe, the other accidents. None of that was planned, was it?

No, not at all!

The Machine digested that.

The other incidents on your shows. That time you were almost shot. The show with the goat's escape. None of those are planned? None of it is staged?

I know it sounds crazy, but no. None of it is.

The Machine . . . felt offended.

This was not the way the world was supposed to work!

How is any of this possible? Why does it keep happening?

I have been Jenn's friend for fifteen years, ever since we were in fifth grade together. And you know what? It's Jenn. She attracts weirdness. She has never known any kind of life that doesn't involve weirdness. To her, it's just normal. It's why she doesn't plan, why she lives minute by minute because she doesn't know any other way to live.

Why?

The next reply was a long time coming.

I have a theory. If I tell you, will you promise to keep it secret? She wouldn't like me telling you, or it getting out.

I shall be discrete.

And he would. In the event he needed to bail on the contract, in the unlikely event he couldn't do his job and boost Jenn's Chopping Spree to award-winning numbers and increase the profit margin by the agreed-upon percentage, then he could easily fabricate a reason to leave.

So, uh, Jenn didn't have the best childhood. It's an old story. Single mom who shouldn't have been a mom in the first place. She took out her stress on Jenn. It was pretty bad.

Abusive?

Oh yeah. She would starve Jenn when Jenn did anything to set her off. And she was pretty easy to set off. When things got really bad, Jenn would stop by our place, and we'd sneak her food. She was so thin.

And now she has her own cooking show.

Yeah. Her mom ran off during high school. Jenn threw us a party to celebrate. Invited us over to her trailer. That's the first time she cooked for anyone. Said her friend helped her prepare it.

Her friend?

She used to have an imaginary friend. It helped her survive her mother and a long string of shitty stepdads, so I never gave her grief about it. You know, kid stuff.

The Machine nodded. The gears in his head were turning now, helping him find sense to this nonsensical woman he'd been forced to work with.

So she was living on her own for a while?

Kind of sort of. She was a teenager, and she didn't have the money to afford the trailer. She bounced around between a couple of friends. And me, mostly. But . . . well, it's Jenn. She draws weirdness to her, and some of it's not good. So while the rest of us were doing college or settling down for the picket fence and 2.5 kids, she was scraping and struggling to get by with three or four ever-shifting part-time jobs and one crisis after another.

I see.

She lives minute to minute because that's how she's always lived. I've tried to get her to get stable, but she doesn't know how. Every time she's tried to control her life, it's fallen to pieces, sometimes in the most ridiculous ways. She's all instinct because it's how she's survived so far. She doesn't plan things through or really thinks about them too much because she doesn't know how.

The Machine considered the situation.

Would it help if I slept with her?

That's a weird question. I didn't think you were the sort to take advantage.

What do you mean?

I mean, I thought her throwing herself at you was a one-sided thing. You seemed to make that pretty clear. So if you pursued her now, it seems to me you'd just be doing it for physical gratification.

The Machine typed.

Oh, I see the reason for your confusion. No, I have no feelings for her. But if it puts her at ease and makes the working relationship more amicable, I believe I could reciprocate. After all, it is her instincts that are driving her towards me, right?

Well . . . yes. It's been a while since the last boyfriend *got kicked out on his ass. That's probably why she's targeting you. But I'm not sure I'm okay with her being used this way.*

It is, in fact, my usage that we are discussing. And I am volunteering it. But if you believe that it would not aid the situation, then I withdraw the consideration.

Hang on. I'm not sure it wouldn't help. Just let me think. She's pretty attractive, you know. She tends to draw a lot of bad boys who are only in it for the sex. But you're saying that's not the driving force with you, here?

The Machine crossed his legs, wincing at the stiffness in his cock. He calculated his response, aware he didn't have much time.

I'd be lying if I said she wasn't attractive. That is a consideration on my part, and any encounter between us wouldn't be one-sided as far as physical pleasure goes. However, a long-term relationship would be impossible. And I must admit that I have no interest in an emotional entanglement. I am horrible at such things.

I actually respect you for that. Um. Well, if you want to give it a try, I know she'd have fun. Just don't hurt her. I know it seems like she's invincible, but she's not. Make her feel good, and make it clear this isn't for the long-term, and you've got my blessing.

Thank you.

The Machine nodded in satisfaction. With that done, he felt the gears engage. A problem had arisen, but logic and planning made the solution clear. He could return to his work without concern and achieve his goal without further complications.

Now let us discuss the Friday show and how I can aid your endeavors.

And they did, for the next hour before he signed off.

But after their talk was done, The Machine's mind turned to Jennifer Doolittle again and the memory of her lips against his.

And he knew he would have no peace until she was in his arms again.

CHAPTER ELEVEN

The North Market is my go-to when the kitchen doesn't cut it.

It's historical and stuff, but none of that really matters to me. What *does* matter is that it's crammed full of food stalls and cooking supply stores. And the food's pretty much the best stuff from a bunch of different ethnic eateries, all the little neighborhoods in the city combining to push chicken croquettes and gyros and gourmet ice cream and pastries.

It's a little pricey, but with the numbers Amy's telling me we hit, I can afford it.

And my sin of choice is ribs—big, heaping slabs of them from the barbecue place, with a sauce that's smokey and sweet at the same time, all dripping grease onto a checked paper-covered basket. I sit on the upstairs balcony, looking down onto the stalls, watching people come and go and shop and consume. A bird flutters among the light fixtures and girders that hold the place together, and I smile at it with sauce-stained teeth.

When I was younger, I used to dream of being a *Disney* princess. Singing and frolicking and calling the animals to me.

It would have been easier than hunting and trapping them, that's for sure. What was his name, Lonny? Lonny the third stepdad? Lonny with a mullet? Yeah, that was him—Lonny, who worked as a varmint control guy on the side and gave me my own trap. I ate a lot better after that for a while, until Momma woke up early and caught me cleaning and dressing that poodle.

The injustice of that beating still stings me. Missus Gruber had six of them. She wouldn't have missed one!

Except she did, and Momma couldn't keep her mouth shut, so we had to move. Again.

It wasn't fair. Besides, poodle tasted horrible. Labradors are where the meat is if you really want a good meal.

Why am I thinking about Momma?

I'm feeling good. Things are going my way. My brain shouldn't be going back there so often.

A flash of black cloth catches my attention, and I look down through the balcony railing to see that the lunch rush has started. Businessmen and women from the surrounding area are coming in to pack their faces with haute and not-so-haughty cuisine. Suits worth more than my entire wardrobe are down there, with fashionably thin people eating themselves fat.

And that makes me think about Curt. Yummy, yummy Curt. He's going to be working with us for at least a few more weeks. I've got that much time to get him in bed or on the sofa or hell, on a floor, if that's what it takes. Except it wouldn't be the floor, he's fussy and particular and would freak out.

It would be fun to watch him freak out.

The chair across from me scrapes, and for a second, I think it's him as a black-suited form sits down. But no, it's Wayne.

"Oh, hey!" I say, grinning. Then I start looking around for Becky. I didn't hear her horsey laugh, which is strange. "Where's your better half?"

"Probably out spending my money." Wayne smiles back. Then he frowns. "Or maybe she's at home spending my money. Fucking *Amazon Prime*."

"Let's be realistic," I say, snapping a rib off and sending sauce splattering really close to Wayne. "If she didn't have that, it'd be the *Home Shopping Network*." I frown. "That's still around, right?"

"Oh yeah. The world could get nuked, and the *Home Shopping Network* would still be there." Wayne chuckles and smooths his hair back.

I bite into the rib, suck the meat off the bone, then notice he doesn't have any food. "Where's your lunch?"

"I haven't gotten it yet." He stares at me. "I just saw you and wanted to say sorry I had to cut and run the day before yesterday."

"Oh, don't worry about it!" I reassure him. I'd forgotten about that. Wayne's not big in my thoughts these days—never was much, to begin with, honestly. I kind of think of him as Becky's accessory, her job, more or less. Kind of like an attachment that lets her stay in debt without any real consequences.

I mean, technically he's the guy who's trying to hunt *her* down so I guess I should be worried, but he sucks at his job, so whatever.

Oops, he's talking again. "Anyway, it looks like I'm going to be pretty busy for the next few days. We're close! I can feel it," he says.

I put the bone next to the others on the black plastic carrier, laying the bones in rows. "Why don't you tell me about it? You seemed pretty excited when you rushed out."

"I shouldn't. This is hush-hush stuff. The word jockeys at the Dispatch would love to hear me spill." He does an exaggerated look around, and I giggle.

He's not really that funny, but it's a better response than telling him he wouldn't have brought it up if he didn't want to talk about it. I think that's the main reason he sat down with me here.

But then Wayne glares at me. "I wasn't joking! This is serious business." He beckons me in close, and I humor him and lean in. He smells like coffee and tobacco and *Vicks VapoRub*.

Blend those all together, and it's not a good smell. Also, his breath is worse.

"Slaughterhouse struck again that day you made chili. Killed a guy just off Sawmill Road! We've been keeping it quiet at the homeowner's request, but the news will report it tonight. And we got a breakthrough!"

"I dunno, Wayne, you've had breakthroughs before." But I can feel my eyes going wide. They weren't supposed to find that guy yet! That was at a private house, and his buddy was traveling!

. . . unless good ol' Chris Devon lied about that. Which he totally would have done, because he *was* that kind of creep.

"What did you find?" I asked. "Fingerprints? Video? A knife left behind or something?"

And now I'm wondering if this is why he's here having lunch with me. If this is some kind of fucked up detective reveal moment.

If he *knows*.

My fingers tighten around one of the meatless ribs. I can probably drive it far enough into his eye to reach his brain.

"A card! Just a shitty little old card with the address of a storage unit on it. Covered in dust that the lab confirmed was quality leather. Somebody kept it in their wallet, and that somebody is Slaughterhouse—why are you laughing?"

I am! I'm shaking and guffawing so hard that other tables are looking at me.

So *that's* where Curt's card got to!

Then I sober up. Yeah, it's funny, but what if he thinks Curt is Slaughterhouse?

That almost sets me off again. Fussy, clean, obsessive-compulsive Curt as a serial killer?

Yeah, right!

Except . . . he did gut that raccoon pretty cleanly. Just snicker-snack, without a flash of worry on his face.

Or anything, really.

I find myself breathing a little heavily. Wayne mistakes my excitement and grins, leans in closer, and keeps talking.

"We're getting the warrant right now. It's over in Spring-field, so we're working with the cops down there. Keeping it on the down-low, so the feds don't get greedy and try to muscle in on our lead. Those assholes in Washington would love to get a jump on us! Make us look like clueless Midwestern assholes."

"Yeah, they're the worst," I whisper back to the clueless Midwestern asshole.

Wayne and I share a laugh. This time no one stares at us. I break off before him to pop another spare rib in my mouth.

His eyes follow my lips as I draw it back, devoid of meat. He swallows, hard, and shakes his head.

"Want some? I've got a nice rack here." I point toward what's left of the ribs.

"I know you do," he fires back. "But I gotta go. Get my ass over to Springfield. The second that warrant clears the wires, we're busting down the door. And even if it's empty, we'll have all the leverage we need to get the records from the rental office."

"Oh. You think Slaughterhouse rented it under her . . . or his real name?"

"If there's one thing I know about Slaughterhouse, it's that he's a real sloppy psycho."

I nod, and sauce drips down my chin.

Wayne nods back, slaps the table, and stands up. "Seeya round, Jenn. Maybe we can do chili night again after we've got that freak in custody." He finger guns at me, and I shake a bone back at him.

After he's gone, I finish my ribs, and I think about that wallet card, and Curt, and the mean, mean trick that's about to happen to him.

For a second, I snigger to myself, imagining them getting

his name and cuffing him and dragging him to the station, with the whole good cop bad cop interrogation thing. Oh, that would piss him off so, so much!

Then I sober up. No. No, he's providing us with *Chopco's* money. And I can't get him into bed if he's in jail. I reach for my phone, and it's missing. I remember it's in the rock quarry lake, probably getting nibbled on by fishes right now.

Fortunately, my apartment's just around the corner. And there's nothing wrong with my laptop.

I fire it up and message Amy. I think about what I want to say. I'm going to have to lie here, since I don't want him to connect the dots from me to *her*. I type.

Hey, do me a favor, okay?

What's wrong?

Nothing's wrong, more or less. I need you to call Curt and let him know that we might have a show opportunity. The police are raiding a storage locker in Springfield. I just got a hot tip that they found a wallet card with Slaughterhouse's secret meat locker listed on it. See if we can rent a similar locker and have a barbecue banquet grill out. Call that show our slasher special or something.

Jesus, Jenn, that's dark. I'm not sure how that'll play.

Just ask him what he thinks. If he hates it, too, we can always do it as a Halloween special or something.

Okay . . . I thought we were pushing it with Chicken and Shrumshrooms, but I can ask.

We should rename it to Shrumshroom and Raccoon.

I've heard worse ideas.

Like cannibal BBQ cookouts in Springfield?

Well, I wasn't gonna say that . . .

I laugh and send her a wave emoji goodbye.

And then I go have a nap. Full belly, after all, and I don't have a show until Friday. Besides, I did a *lot* of running around back on Monday. Time for some well-earned rest!

CHAPTER TWELVE

N o rest for the weary, The Machine thought to himself as he sped down I-70.

He was on his way to Springfield, going above the speed limit—only nine mph above—with *Waze* open on his phone to warn him of police speed traps.

The Machine used to put his trust in radar detectors, but the technology had fallen behind long ago. Now there was an app for that, and it did its job well as the sweat rolled down his forehead, and his *Camaro* roared down the road, past orange barrels and long-haul semis alike.

And as he went, one question rolled around in his mind, the gears chewing at it, again and again, trying to catch, trying to break down the problem and come to an answer.

How?

Fact—His wallet card had gone missing Sunday night, most likely dropped at Schmidt's during the disastrous *date*.

Fact—The card contained the address and keycode for his storage locker in Springfield.

Fact—Jenn—*The Diva* had gotten wind that the cops were investigating Slaughterhouse's storage locker. In Springfield.

Fact—If *The Diva* was to be believed, they had gotten this information from a wallet card.

The Machine did not believe in coincidences. Even the weirdness on that quarry lake island had all been reasonable, in hindsight. It was an unsafe operational environment, and they had not taken the appropriate precautions to deal with raccoon-infested areas.

There were no coincidences.

The most likely explanation was that the card had found its way to the police somehow.

But *how?*

Theory one — Someone at the restaurant had picked up the card and turned it in to the police, claiming that it was an artifact related to Slaughterhouse.

Theory two — A police officer had picked up the card and mistaken it for an artifact related to Slaughterhouse.

Theory three — Slaughterhouse had been at the restaurant and left the card somewhere the police would find it.

Theory four — The Diva was messing with him. She had dangled the card in front of her police detective acquaintance.

Theory one was a possibility. The Diva's aggression had created an unseemly incident, and he had been put off-balance, possibly acted in a manner that could be associated with a criminal sociopath. It was possible for a sharp person to see the card left behind as a clue. Particularly with the city in a panic over Slaughterhouse's latest kill. Some armchair detective could have forwarded it to the police.

It was a slight possibility, as it went. But it was there.

The same possibility applied to theory two. The armchair detective was, in that case, a police officer of some sort who had been in the restaurant and picked up the card.

Theory three . . . that was unlikely. Possible, but unlikely. The odds that Slaughterhouse would be in the same restaurant at roughly the same time as The Machine were astronomical. Serial killers were a rare breed, to begin with, and the odds that two active and free members of this peculiar lifestyle would share a room at any given time . . . no, the possibility was too remote to be considered.

Which left theory four, The Diva was playing a practical joke on him.

She was sending him to Springfield for some inscrutable

reason, perhaps setting up to *prank* him once he got onsite.

That was the most possible reason.

The gears ground, and he was forced to admit that this was probably the reality of the situation, which eased his tension somewhat. Yes, the drive out here was required. There was a non-zero chance of some of the nature of his work being revealed. That could lead to problems down the line. But it was unlikely to end in disaster, and the odds were that he would arrive out here to find nothing out of order, and no inconvenience beyond a quick half-hour trip back to Columbus.

The thought comforted him, and he slowed his speed a bit, switching from *Waze* to his Internet radio station. Finding the song he wanted, he let *Blackstreet* tell him exactly how much diggity was tolerable. *The answer's none. There's always no diggity allowed.*

The good feeling lasted until he was driving up to the gate to the *U-Stor-It* lot and saw the police car parked next to the office.

Without hesitation, The Machine stopped, put the car into reverse, and headed back the way he'd come.

Passing by the gothic and looming form of a masonic hall, The Machine found a parking lot and idled, collecting his thoughts.

The distant, comforting possibility that theory four was the correct one faded by the second.

Fortunately, The Machine had a fallback plan for this sort of eventuality. The geography of this part of Springfield had a few hills and points of elevation to work with.

The Machine speed-dialed the motel overlooking the rear of the *U-Stor-It* and rented room 106. Then he drove over, took his emergency bag from the trunk, checked in, and entered his room.

Changing into casual clothes, jeans and a t-shirt, he took out binoculars and studied the lot from the window. Room 106 had a perfect vantage point, one he'd personally verified years ago.

Springfield had lost most of its major companies long ago. The rustbelt had done a number on the limited industry in the area, and the local economy had never really recovered.

So, when he examined the rusty fence at the back of the lot, he was gratified to find that the loose section he'd noticed years ago was still in place. No one had bothered to replace it. Any money that might have done so had likely gone up the proprietor's nose.

The next obstacle was the security cameras.

The Machine trained the binoculars over to the freestanding poles with the obvious boxes wired to them. Then down to where the cables snaked across to the main building.

He couldn't get the footage. But he could prevent the footage from showing him in the first place.

A glance over showed the police arguing with a large man in a Hawaiian shirt. Probably the storage employee on duty. They weren't in the enclosed part of the storage yet, so he had a little time to work.

The Machine unzipped his emergency bag and dug in it until he found what he was looking for—an ancient set of lawn darts. On went his gloves, and he tucked the lawn darts under his arm as he descended the stairs, out of the hotel.

It took three tries to huck the heavy dart over the fence and into the cluster of cables at the base of the nearest pole. He knew he'd done it properly when fat sparks snapped up, and the lights on the camera's box winked off.

Then it was through the loose section of the fence and back among the storage containers. He retrieved the lawn darts as he went, tucking them into his waistband. A tap on the keypad later, and his storage unit was open before him.

Compared to many other units around here, the contents were innocuous—six cardboard boxes, each the size of a footstool. Four were empty. Two were sealed. All were stamped

Mendelson's in capital letters, the black ink faded and worn from the march of time.

And in the back corner, a set of propane tanks, with a blowtorch next to them.

Time was short, but The Machine felt a tug at him. Felt the gears clicking, for once his higher brain in accord with his instincts. He opened the first sealed box and stared down into the Styrofoam packing peanuts. He reached in and came up with a small thing.

A brass pocket watch. One of thirty-six in that cardboard crate.

Mendelson's had been a warehouse liquidation store, a business down in Dayton that had bought up lots of random machinery and goods from other stores that bulk-sold them to make some profit from their loss. In its heyday, it had occupied an eight-story building in the middle of the crumbling remnants of the Dayton downtown area.

The Machine had found it back during his troubled years, back when he was aimless and just Curt, not the engine he had made of himself now. Before he had a purpose, in those formless proto years, he had struggled, knowing something was wrong with the world but unable to figure out just what it was or how to fix it.

The cramped, twisting corridors of Mendelson's upper floors had matched the state of his mind. Dusty, with crates full of old and forgotten goods to either side, they had neither order nor memory to them. They changed as the store's acquisition personnel brought in new items, and dumped them wherever they could find room.

Once, a man The Machine had known had picked through there and found a set of *Zeiss* camera lenses that were worth thousands of dollars, purchased for pennies, more or less. But the majority of it was junk. There were vacuum tubes for computers whose total production run didn't hit double digits, pipe fittings for pipes which had gone out of usage during the Truman administration, and things more esoteric and bizarre.

It was there, in the darkness and un-airconditioned heat of the heart of the stacks that the man who would become The Machine had found them.

Six crates. Thirty-six watches per crate. Sitting there oiled, in *Styrofoam*. Blank and oiled and perfect, waiting to be engraved for retirees of a company that had folded or moved on decades ago.

The Machine had not been wealthy at the time. But he had purchased the whole lot of them for three hundred dollars and counted himself lucky.

And back in his cheap apartment, with the smell of marijuana wafting in from the neighboring rooms, and the sound of the downstairs meth-head beating his wife, the lost young man who was Curt had lifted up the first watch. And listening to wordless whispers, feeling the rightness of it, he had pried open the case and studied the gears, tweezing them out with fine tools and studying just how they went together, looking them over, feeling them, knowing what they signified, and staring at them night and day until he could feel the gears in his own brain. The ones that slowly, ever so slowly, started to turn.

The ones that told him that the meth-head downstairs needed to be removed from the world to improve it.

Curt had made his first mask then, sewing the gears and components onto the leather from an old, worn coat that he'd kept for no reason.

That first mask was also the last mask that Curt had ever made.

Because when he was done, Curt put on the mask.

But The Machine was the one who took it off after the deed was done and the meth-head lay bleeding and dead.

What had his name been? It didn't matter. The Machine

had concentrated and found the best way to dispose of the body. And after that, whenever he went to sleep at night, there were no more sounds of fists beating flesh, no woman screaming and whimpering for mercy. The gears moved in his mind, turning smoothly, powering him forward into the future.

And the world was a better place — for a time.

A gear clicked in The Machine's mind, and he slid the watch into his pocket. He had little time for this reminiscence.

Voices came to his ears, and he froze.

Someone was moving on the other side of the wall, talking loudly. A voice he recognized.

"Shit, they only have numbers on half of these," the detective said. The one that The Machine had met a few nights ago, at The Diva's chili dinner. "Murkowski, you want to go left?"

"Not really," a different man said. "I've seen enough *Scooby-Doo* to know splitting up never works."

"You'd get to say jinkies. Jinkies is cool."

"I'm more of a Daphne man. Dem tights . . . mmmm . . ."

"Perv. Thick nerds are where it's at — " The detective broke off as a tinny rendition of *Sir Mix-A-Lot's* seminal song declared his love for ponderous posteriors. "Shit. I need to take this. You go ahead."

"Yeah, no. I'll wait right here. *Away* from any dark alleys. Or hidden murder corners."

"Hello? Wait. What? The feds? A task force? Interpol? Are you fucking with me?"

The Machine saw his chance. He looked between the two cardboard boxes and shook his head.

No. The extra watches were a necessary sacrifice at this juncture.

Carefully, he crept over to the blowtorch, made sure it was lined up with the propane tank, averted his eyes as instructed, and brought it to crackling life.

"You hear something?" the detective's partner asked.

Then The Machine ran for his life.

Shouts from behind.

Shouts that were eclipsed as the air turned warm on his back, and a devil's wind blew across him.

Whump!

The desk clerk was out of the motel and staring across the field as The Machine ran past him. "Whoa," the guy said, pupils wide and dilated, blinking in the harsh light of the fire. "Dude, did you see that?"

"Yes," The Machine said and closed the door behind him. He got behind the front desk, grabbed the hard drive of the clerk's computer, did a quick check for security cameras, then headed upstairs. Two minutes later, he was packed and in his car and taking a leisurely route away that bypassed the flashing lights of the emergency response vehicles.

It was a short drive back to Columbus, but The Machine felt the gears sliding together.

Even *before* they had gotten into the storage unit, the police had been talking about federal and international involvement. That overheard conversation boded ill.

The Machine knew he was not finished.

Only one question remained. How far would he have to go before he was done?

CHAPTER THIRTEEN

"Got a question for you," I tell Curt. "How far are you willing to go here?"

There's a pause, and I regret that I can't see his face. I'm calling him from my new phone. It's an android, so it and Curt have so much in common.

"You're going to have to provide some context here," killjoy Curt tells me.

"All right, okay. So uh, *Buca's* ended up dropping us after all."

"Unacceptable. Let me make a few phone calls."

"No, no, well, yes. You can if you want. That would make Amy happy if you sicced *Chopco* on them. But this gives us a problem for tomorrow's show. We're going to have to fall back to a different idea. I had one that tied in local events and interest, but, uh . . . well, the place caught on fire."

"You're talking about the meat locker."

The meat locker is what the press has dubbed the crime scene over in Springfield. Well, the most recent crime scene over in Springfield. Well . . . okay, the one that involves Slaughterhouse. Maybe. There's a storage place down there that's been cordoned off, and some seriously suited people are showing up in black SUVs. The local news is torn between speculating about secret alien autopsy remains and the FBI having Slaughterhouse cornered in there.

I'm pretty sure it's not the last one. But my best lead on that is being treated for second-degree burns right now. Becky won't shut up about it, and she's been over to my apartment

114

three or four times to wail and yell about how hard it is on her. That's probably two or three times more than she's visited her husband in the hospital.

"Hello?" Curt asks.

"Right! Sorry. Yeah, we had something lined up around the meat locker, but well."

"Well."

"You're curt today." I snicker. "But then you're Curt every day." Damn, I'm in a good mood! I should be writing these down. I'm not sure what that wallet card was, but there's no doubt in my mind he pulled some strings to have some corporate hitters burn the evidence down. I hope it worked. We need him for at least another week or so.

At his long-suffering sigh, I decide to stop playing and get to the point. "Aaaaaaannnyway, we have another location. But it's over in the Hocking Hills."

"I'm unfamiliar with that place."

"I thought you were from Cincinnati?"

"I've lived there for years. Why, are these Hills nearby?"

"They're in between Cincinnati and Athens. A little northish."

"I think that's why I didn't know about them. There's nothing between Cincinnati and Athens."

"There's hills! And trailers. And meth. So much meth . . . but no, Hocking's different. I mean, there's probably meth, but there's hiking trails and Amish and about a billion little cabins."

"And you have a tie-in recipe for that area?"

"Yep! We're going to make whoopie pies with a wood stove!"

"I'm afraid to ask."

"Don't be." I grin. "Take two hand-sized chunks of cake, put a ton of cream-based icing between them. It's an Amish desert, the sort of thing you can only enjoy guilt-free if you've been yodering it up in the fields all day and burning calories like a bonfire."

"I'm not sure how this is going to fly with the healthy-obsessed demographic that watches you."

"They've got plenty of other shows of ours that do healthy stuff. This one's for a guilty pleasure."

"Has your technical director been working the details?"

I correct him, trying not to sound too snippy. "Yes. *Amy* has." Why the hell can't he ever remember her name?

"Good. I'll check with her for the details." He hangs up.

I bite my lip. He's been no fun ever since I told him about Springfield.

Well, at least he's got nothing to worry about from the police. *He's* not the one they're chasing right now.

But I'd be happier if he stopped being such a poop.

Fortunately, Amy says she has matters well in hand, there. I'm not sure how, but I trust her judgment.

I trust her judgment a little less an hour later when we're piling everything into Curt's car. The scowl on his face could curdle milk at twenty paces.

"You're certain this is the most efficient way?"

"Yes, it is," Amy tells him. She's so cute when she's got her *determined* look on. "Even with the line of credit, you know the budget we're operating with. Until we prove we can keep the numbers either growing or steady, we can't take the risk of a really big bill. Whereas you, you've got a different expense line. So long as you're the primary transportation and bill-payer here, you can charge damn near anything and they won't screw you over if the numbers tank."

"That only works until it doesn't," Curt warns. "There are limits."

"Oh please," I break in. "It's not like we're spending lavishly and doing cocaine off the backs of hookers. This is *Ohio.*

This'll be a cheap trip."

I see a shifty look in his eyes. He's totally done cocaine off the backs of hookers. Hookerback? Is that a proper word? I don't know. I don't ask him.

He argues a little more but gives in after the third suitcase is packed. And then we're on the road.

I've got the backseat directly behind Curt, and I'm studying him as we drive. Amy's riding shotgun, since she knows where we're going.

I didn't bother asking where we're going. I don't want to bother learning the name of someplace like Turkey Leg Road or Bob's Barn Byway or whatever the hell rural shit is out here.

Half an hour later, I'm rethinking my stance as we're eating lunch at an honest to god fifties-style diner, silver-bullet shaped and with the most decadent burgers I've had in a long time. My teeth snap through the meat and vegetable-bits, and juice runs down my chin. Curt stares as I devour the first one and reach for the next. His own has like a single bite in it.

"Sfgood," I say, trying not to spray him.

"Evidently. Not the sort of place I'm used to." The inside is a bit cramped. The windows overlook a permanent flea market and a mini-mall full of antique stores.

"Antiques are a big thing out here. Some of them are maybe even real," I say. "Mostly the old farm stuff and the worthless crap."

"Unreal antiques?" Curt quirks an eyebrow. With the light behind him the way it is, it catches his face just right, seems to make it glow. Makes it look like his eyebrows are on fire.

There are worse ways to burn to death, really. His other eyebrow goes up, and I realize that I've trailed off. "Oh yeah. Counterfeit antiques are big business," I confirm. "People buy new furniture and generic-looking things, and weather and wash them to make it look like they've been around forever.

Didn't you ever see *Antiques Roadshow*?"

"In fact, I haven't. My particular line of business has never intersected with that market."

"Jenn used to do it as a sideline," Amy says, not looking up from her map.

Curt does a double-take. "What? Why?"

"Money!" I say, stealing some of Amy's fries as vengeance. She doesn't notice. "And it's a victimless crime."

"Keep your voice down," he says, looking around.

There's an elderly couple who are staring and glaring, but nobody else in here cares. And they could be glaring at us because we're young, or because I just ate two burgers, and they can't eat one without their diabetes flaring up or something like that.

"It isn't a victimless crime," Curt says, and it's my turn to quirk an eyebrow at him. At least I think that's what I'm doing. It's hard to tell. I've never tried before.

"Totally victimless," I say, finishing my second burger in a few bites.

"How is it, victimless? You ripped your customers off."

"Point of order," I say, jabbing a ketchup-smeared finger at him. "I had no customers. I was a supplier to someone who did. So, it's not on *me*. I just made the stuff."

"You still enabled fraud. You were an accomplice. There were *victims*."

"Nope! Nobody who buys antiques is a victim. There are two types."

"Two types of victims."

"Shoosh," I tell him, waving my milkshake. It hasn't brought any boys to the yard yet, but the day is young. "There are two types. There's the rich re-seller, who is hoping to rip off some old toothless geezer and steal their prized possession for pennies. Those guys can afford losses, and if they can't, fuck 'em. They tried to trick Old Ethel! They deserve what they get."

"Ethel."

"Rhetorical Ethel. Doesn't actually exist Ethel."

The old woman's giving me an even sour-er look. Pretty sure her name's Ethel.

"And the other type?" Curt asks, folding his hands. They're near to mine, and I fight the urge to grab them. Good bones in those hands. Broad, smooth, perfectly manicured. His hand would feel like old leather, like good leather, like *her* face.

"The other type," I say, fighting my mind back to business, "The other type is people who wouldn't care if it was real or not."

"How could they not? The whole point of an antique is to be authentic."

"No," I say, putting my milkshake down. "The whole point is that they *think* it's authentic. They bought it to pull the whole room together or to look at it and feel the weight of history. They bought the thingy because it made them happy. That's why. And if they don't dig too hard, then they never find out it's fake. So it's a non-issue."

"That's how a lot of relationships work," Amy breaks in, unexpectedly. I glance over to her, and she's smiling, the light catching her glasses and making her look all anime. "The people involved know not to dig too far, and so they stay happy."

"To ignorance!" I raise my milkshake in a mock toast. "It's bliss!"

And to my surprise, Curt clacks his old-timey coke glass cup against my milkshake. He offers a smile, even! And his face doesn't break! "To ignorance," he says, and throws back his H2O. "It's so very profitable."

"So . . . you're not getting on me for fraud anymore?" I ask, a little amazed.

"No. You put forward a good case. Until and unless it's

disproved, I think you're right."

"Oh. Uh. Wow. Okay."

It's stupid.

His approval feels good.

And I think I'm blushing.

A flash of light in the corner of my vision, and I see Amy looking away, smirking. She lifts the map up quickly, cutting off my view of her face. But not soon enough!

Everyone in the diner jumps when I slam my hand onto the table, and the plates rattle. "Okay! Let's hit the road. We've got a show to do!"

Things go smoothly after that.

Smoother than I'm used to.

We get back in the hills, past the washboard-adorned cutesy corner shops that sell moonshine and camping supplies, and drive past countless roads stuck on hills at angles that would flip a semi-truck. Our cabin is a fairly nice business, complete with all the rustic comforts such as air conditioning and a hot tub. It's got a back porch that looks out over a pond, and it's all by itself.

"You could sink a ton of bodies in that," I say, leaning on the deck and staring at the cattails surrounding the water.

"They wouldn't stay sunk," Curt says, leaning in next to me, suit whispering as it rides up his arms. Not far, they're pretty muscular. "Too shallow. One good drought, and they'd be visible for the next set of weekenders."

"Not if you ground them up first. I see fish! Give it a month, and they'd eat all the evidence."

"Oh my God, morbid much?" Amy asks. "That's just bad taste, with all this Slaughterhouse stuff going on. Come on, help me move all this in."

I help her out, and it goes well until the last trunk Curt's hauling has a latch break open, and what looks like a bunch of colonial re-enactment garb falls on the ground.

"What the hell is this?" I ask as I haul up something you'd see in Little House on the Prairie.

"Amish recipe, Amish costumes," Amy grins, holding up suspenders and a straw hat.

"Wait. Costumes? Plural?" Curt asks, looking alarmed.

I grin as I pull out a fake beard. "C'mon, Ezekiel, we got a barn needs raising!"

"No. Absolutely not!" Curt says, folding his arms.

Twenty minutes later he's garbed up and helping me stir the batter in an earthenware bowl, while I natter at the camera and fiddle with my bonnet.

Well, at least he's got the no-smiling part down! I think that's an Amish thing. Maybe. Who knows?

The wood stove takes longer than expected to cook up the batter, and more firewood than expected. I send Curt out with an ax, and he comes back half-soaked and looking even more sour. "It's raining."

"Yeah?" I sneak a look outside at the darkening sky. "Whoa. That looks nasty."

"It is." He puts soggy wood in the stove, and we get some seriously damp puffs of steam out of it. Then I see Amy waving her hand and mouthing words at me. That's our signal!

"Time to go to break! We'll be back when the exciting part's ready!" I chirp into the camera. It's a new one, smaller and with higher resolution and better tech stuff. I swear Amy got flushed talking about all the stats earlier.

"Clear!" Amy announces and then plugs the camcorder into the wall to charge.

Ba-boom!

The cabin goes dark.

"Oh," I say, as the power trips back on. "Just a close lightning stroke—"

Kroom!!!!

This time it stays dark.

Curt coughs.

"Yeah, okay," I say slowly. "This is a problem . . ."

"Give me one minute," he says and heads back outside.

I count, just to be contrary.

And at fifty-eight seconds, he struggles back inside, hauling a small crate.

"What is that?" Amy asks.

"Portable generator," he says, simply.

"Wait. What? You just have one of those in your car?" I burst out.

"You don't?" Curt asks.

The bad news is that it's not powerful enough to keep the whole cabin going for long.

The good news is that we don't *need* the whole cabin. We're cooking on a wood stove! All we need to do is keep Amy's rig powered and get enough of a Wi-Fi boost to keep the stream streaming. Amy does stuff I don't understand, then shoots me a thumbs up, and I put on my game face again and bury my hands in the chocolate-flavored dough.

"Welcome back! We had some technical difficulties, but now the dough's firmed up, and it's *chopping time!*"

I slice the roll of dough like a sausage, popping the rounds onto the baking pan. Already greased up with bacon fat, the cake does its thing. The end result is something like a fluffier brownie. They don't take long to rise, and less time to cool after they're off the stove.

"And now for the cream de la cream!"

I see Curt wince, and I grin wide at him as I scoop out gobs of the white stuff with a wooden spoon and ladle it onto the slabs of cake. Then one slab goes on top of another, and you've got a gooey, cake-ish version of an *Oreo* the size of both my fists.

It tastes every bit as decadent as it looks.

We close the show out with an American Gothic looking

pose. Without the pitchfork, since we forgot to bring one.

"All right." Amy yawns, once we're clear and the show is a wrap. "Well, that took a long time. I'll take the smaller bedroom. Have a good night!"

"Wait. What?" My voice sounds strange, and then I realize that Curt and I said it simultaneously.

"I didn't tell you?" Amy asks. "We've got the cabin for the night. We're staying here and leaving in the morning."

"No, you didn't." Curt frowns. "Give me one good reason I shouldn't pack up the car right now."

"I'll give you several," Amy says. "By the contractual agreements between you, the subcontractor, and *Chopco's* expense department, we would have to file twenty forms to cancel this expense. And since this cabin has a no-cancellation clause, *Chopco* would have to dispute it with them. The resulting legal tangle would *not* reflect well on any of us, including you."

Curt's mouth is open in a perfect *O*.

Amy continues, mercilessly. "Two! It's past my contractual working hours, and riding back with you would be a breach of my contract. I would technically be on the job and thus working over-time, which is strictly against my rules. You want to ask me to bend the rules here?"

Curt's mouth is closed shut now, and he's glaring.

"Three! I called up your partner Randall and got his blessing. I'll text you the message now."

Now Curt's jaw is loose, and I'm laughing. "She's got you, Curt! She's got you! You can't escape her when she's like this! Just give in . . . to the powers of the Amy side!"

Curt looks at the heavy frying pan. And my knives. And for a second, for a split-second, there's something in his face that makes my knees wobble, and my heart skips a beat.

"All right," Curt says, slowly, as he pulls the fake beard off his face. "I guess you've got me."

I keep laughing, but now I'm wondering.
The night is young.
Why is she doing this? What is Amy's game here?

CHAPTER FOURTEEN

"That's a hotel on Park Place," The Machine announced, putting the small, red plastic token down as he swept away four smaller green tokens.

Then he leveled his gaze at the mousy woman across the board, as the candlelight danced and shuddered.

Monopoly was her game, as it turned out. It had been a long time since he had been this challenged in anything even vaguely related to a business venture.

The Diva sulked on the side, looking from her meager stack of money to the few property cards she had left. Everything else had been divided between The Machine and the technical director—the very manipulative and underhanded technical director.

He'd seriously considered killing her when she sprang the little surprise with the cabin on them, but given the force of the storm out there and the questionable road quality between this location and his hotel, he was forced to agree that some level of caution was required.

And it would be an improper death. The Machine did *not* act on impulse, which was why he was still in the game.

The technical director smirked and rolled the dice. The Machine watched her inch closer to Park Place . . . and then beyond it. "There's my two hundred," she said, and The Machine peeled off the play money, and handed it over.

He'd only agreed to play after they let him be the banker. It gave him some small amount of satisfaction, of control.

The Diva had no such satisfaction. She rolled, moved her

car to Free Parking, then glared daggers at the other two play-
ers. "I could have turned this around if we'd done the money
on Free Parking thing!"

"Jenn. No," the technical director said. "That's the number
one mistake. If you do that, then games take *forever*."

"The rules are clear," The Machine said, rolling the dice.
He frowned as he moved his top hat to Baltic Avenue and
paid the technical director the modest amount. The roll was
within tolerances but would put some strain on his next turn.
That hotel had stretched him thin.

And then the technical director rolled an eleven.

She looked from her thimble to St. Charles Place.

And the hotel on it.

"Fuck."

"Fuck," The Machine agreed. "Payment, please."

She was shuffling through her deeds, trying to figure out
what to mortgage, when the lights snapped back on. The microwave in the little kitchenette beeped, and the smoke detec-
tor wailed.

"That should really have a battery," The Machine re-
marked. "It's against code otherwise."

"Right. I think I'm out," the technical director said and did
a long stretch, yawning. "Off to bed for me. Play nice, kids."

"I'm older than you are," The Machine reminded her.

"Yep. Kick his ass, Jenn."

"Nah, this game sucks," The Diva said. "I'm heading for
the hot tub. You want to give it a try?" Her gaze found The
Machine.

"Absolutely," The Machine said, as he packed the battered
board game away. "Do let me know when you're finished."

She glared at him and stalked off.

The Machine was in his room, typing up an expense report
on his laptop, when the door creaked open.

"She was asking you to join her," the technical director whispered.

"What?" The Machine looked up. "Who was . . . oh. Hm."

"And she didn't pack any bathing suits."

"Neither did I."

"Do the math," the technical director said and slid the door shut again.

Some quick mental arithmetic later, a warm heat pulsed through him as he felt himself stiffen.

His earlier conversation with the technical director ran through his mind. And he wondered how long it had taken her to set this scenario up.

It didn't matter. She had been a . . . wingman. Yes, that was the term.

The Machine put aside his laptop, stripped down, examined himself in the bathroom's small mirror, and threw a towel around his waist. His cock, freed from the restraint of pants, bobbed and dipped in anticipation.

It had been a long time, now that he thought of it. Perhaps that was why he felt anticipation throbbing in his chest and in his groin. Perhaps that was why he opened the door and moved to the deck.

And yet, he hesitated.

He recalled her face at the restaurant — her eyes.

She was a liar.

Why had he said that?

He felt his cock deflating, felt stiffness loosen.

And then he heard a giggle from outside.

The Machine looked up to see her in the tub, staring through the glass at him. She was naked in the bubbling and roiling tub, and her breasts swayed as she waved at him. Her nipples were spots of pink in the light of the deck, berries on cream.

The Machine felt his manhood stir again and stepped through the door. He clutched the towel to him with one hand

and shut the door behind him, sliding the glass on its metal rail.

"Finally worked up the nerve?" she whispered, her voice barely audible above the sound of the rain. It was warm and loud, and it pattered on the overhang above the hot tub. Without a word, The Machine let his towel slide down.

Her gaze slid down, and the corners of her mouth curled up as he slid in.

"I was expecting it to be smaller," she said.

"I'm happy to exceed your expectations," he said, staring at her from four feet away.

A brush, skin sliding along his foot and up his leg, he snapped his hand down, caught her foot as it tried to slide into his lap.

She giggled.

He caressed her foot, and she gasped as he ran his fingers around the toes, squeezing them with his palm. Then he slid his hand up her ankle, running her calf through the cage of his fingers, up and down, feeling the slight catch of sharpness.

"I . . . haven't shaved today," she said, out of breath for the first time, looking a little flustered.

"That's fine," he whispered and slid closer, around the side so he could bring his other arm into play.

He found her shoulder, tensed and hard, and ran his hand up her collarbone, felt her trembling neck. He caressed it, fingers in back with tips just touching her spine, thumb rubbing up and down, up to her chin as she shuddered and heaved at the sensation —

"No," she whispered, low and guttural.

"No?" The Machine stopped.

"Now *you're* lying!" she snarled.

Pain and impact.

She hit me, he realized as his head rocked back.

"You're doing it wrong!" she screamed, and then she was on

him, biting and clawing, hands scrabbling to pin him as she grunted and panted.

The Machine fought for his life.

He shoved her, twisted, tried to slam her head into the side of the tub, but his hand slipped from her skull as she turned and latched her jaw into his collarbone. He grunted in pain, and she pinned his left hand against the tub with incredible strength. She scrambled on top of him, legs wrapping around him as he pounded her back with his remaining free hand, trying to grab for her hair and missing as she pulled her bloody mouth free and slammed her skull into his.

More pain, a flash of light, and then her fingers clawed at his side, trying to dig between them.

And he realized she was going for his cock.

This wasn't an assault.

This was *foreplay.*

The Machine felt the gears hum to life, and for the first time tonight, he found himself interested.

Oh, he'd been hard before. But that was just the attraction of his body.

Now his brain was engaged. This was going to be more than rutting.

This was going to be about violence, about abuse.

This was about *hurting.*

The realization came too late for the first struggle. He felt her fingers wrap around his length, and before he could turn matters around, she shifted, and he gasped as he felt himself slide into her.

She gasped back, inches from his face, the smell of his own blood wafting into his mouth as she moaned.

The Machine slipped his hand free from her pin, wrapped his arms around her waist, and *stood,* driving himself to the hilt in her cunt, feeling her pubic hair tickle along his own. Pressure and heat, searing heat along his cock, the head of it feeling as if it was on fire as he stood upright in the tub.

For a second, she hung, paralyzed and impaled.

Then he felt her legs dig further around his waist, and her arms whip around his shoulders. She laughed, and she bounced on his cock, bracing against him to drive herself up and down, the wet slapping of her flesh against his filling the air.

The Machine slipped.

He staggered, trying to recover, and she growled, then bit his cheek as he bellowed.

He twisted as he fell, and they tumbled out of the tub together, hitting the deck, feeling the wood against his elbow and forearm as she gasped, stunned. She lay there, legs spread, and he took the lead, driving himself in like a hammer driving a nail as she lay supine beneath him.

Then she snapped out of it, eyes glaring up at him as she howled, bucking and writhing and trying to escape his impaling cock.

But . . . she wasn't. His razor-sharp mind saw she'd bypassed some opportunities. She was struggling, but not to her full capabilities.

And he started to understand the rules of this game.

So when she snarled and slammed her palm into the side of his head, he pretended it had stunned him, let her flip over and ride him, hips pumping, pushing him deeper into her cunt, ass slamming against his thighs as she gasped and sighed. He let her go for a minute, and she came then, warm walls clamping around him like a closing fist, a gush of wetness down his shaft, soaking his balls. She opened her mouth, but no sound came out . . . and in the silence, he grabbed her, pulled her off him. She struggled, but she was weaker, riding the pleasure, and he slammed her down with her breasts on the edge of the tub and her ass in the air.

She could have kicked him then.

But she let him plant a hand on her spine just above her ass, and with his other hand pushing her chest down, he drove himself into her swollen, gaping pussy from behind. He took his time with this, watching the head disappear and hearing her wail, sensitive still from her last orgasm. Only when the smooth, trimmed stubble of his pubes were tickling her labia did he pause.

They stopped, locked together.

She struggled, whipping her arms back to claw at him, and he lay on her, abs folding over her ass cheeks, as he shifted his grip to her hair.

And then he rocked, pulling out a good four inches and slamming his cock back in, watching her ass wobble with every impact. She wailed but took it, and he let go for a second to bring his open palm down on her right cheek with a *crack*.

She screamed, and he pumped, pumped, pumped her relentlessly, as the heat rose within his balls, and he felt his shaft grow sensitive, feeling the warmth clamp around him as she drew close herself.

He came that way, buried in her from behind, biting her shoulder as she growled. He sprayed into her, spurting his seed into her hot, slippery depths as she jerked and writhed, then relaxed around him like warm jello.

They fell limp next to the hot tub, blood dripping down their bodies to pool on the floor, spunk oozing from their genitals, and water everywhere.

Silence, as the rain fell from above. A low roll of thunder, rumbling elsewhere.

But neither of them spoke. They didn't want to break the moment.

CHAPTER FIFTEEN

Amy's smirking at me, and normally I'd be pissed but whatever. Right now, I'm just feeling too good to be irked.

Sore, but good.

We're sitting at a far table in the back of the *Olde Dutch Restaurant* or something like that, chowing down on a really decadent buffet. Seriously good fried chicken! Curt's just gotten up for seconds, and now Amy's barely-there poker face slips, and she leers at me.

"Well?" she asks, and the word hangs in the air between us.

I make measurements with my hands, and she grins lewdly. Then she sobers up. "You've got a lot of band-aids on you."

"Yep. So does he, his clothes just cover more." I'm in a halter top and shorts. He's in slacks and a polo shirt. It's simple geometry.

More like geography, now that I think of it. Abs bulgier than those hills around us right now, mmmm . . .

"Okay, so that was all consensual last night? Because it sounded kind of like murder, and the collateral damage looked like a crime scene," Amy tells me.

"No, it was nothing like a crime scene," I say absent-mindedly. My memory has drifted south of those abs.

"What?"

"What?" I ask her back.

"Okay. I just wanted to make sure he wasn't another

Trent."

"Oh, he's not." Trent was far too stringy to do much with beyond sausages. Curt is well-marbled steaks at least—a wave of revulsion hits me, and I don't know why. I belch, feel my fried chicken trying to come up, and grab for a napkin. It's a struggle, but I keep it down.

"Oh shit! I'm sorry, Jenn." Amy reaches across and grabs my shoulder. "Sorry, sorry, I know he's a sore memory."

A sore memory that gave me stitches. Trent went upside my head with a tire iron once. But *she* took care of him. Even the strongest asshole has to sleep sometime, and he didn't wake up.

"He's long gone, off in another state. Lots of alimony to dodge there, y'know?" I get my gorge under control, and Amy squeezes my shoulder, then looks up.

Curt sits next to me, and I lean into him. He stiffens, then accepts it. I steal a few carrots off his plate, and he gets less accepting, scooting the thing away from me.

"You have your own," he tells me.

"Yeah, but yours is tastier," I purr. "And so's your food."

Amy gets very busy with her blackberry cobbler, trying to pretend she isn't paying attention.

Curt sighs. I straighten up and let him eat but keep my arm across his shoulders. They're broad shoulders. Very good at hugging or holding me down while I come around him. Flexible, y'know?

We finish up our meal and walk through the gift shop, declining to buy any number of kitschy, cutesy, farm-related items. Though Amy does scoop up and purchase an armful of no-bake cookies, the size of small plates.

It's an exploitable weakness. I'll remember it for later.

Curt drives us back home, and this time I've got shotgun. I study him with maximum side-eye as we go.

Why did I call you a liar?

I'd gone into that tub hoping for a pleasant night, hoping

to get an itch scratched.

But something . . . something about how he'd touched me infuriated me.

Not in a bad way, just . . .

He'd been holding back. That was what *she* thought. He'd been holding back.

Yeah. That was it.

He'd come prepared to make love, but I'd wanted to *fuck*.

I hadn't known I'd wanted it that way.

I've never jumped someone like I jumped on him.

Never cut loose.

And it was *good*. I still felt the ache up inside me, the throbbing warmth of my lower lips against my panties.

"I want to do that again soon," I tell him as soon as I think it.

I hear plastic crinkling in the back seat, glance up into the mirror to see that Amy's suddenly gotten very interested in her cookies. She's smiling, though.

"I've got a lot of work to catch up on tonight," Curt says, after a moment. "But tomorrow's open. We could take a walk and—"

"Or we could skip the walk and fuck. Over and over again," I say.

He clears his throat and glances up to the mirror. "This is mixed company."

"It's Amy. She doesn't count."

"Mmfscuse me?" she says through a mouth of chocolate-coated oats.

"You know what I mean. Go back to your cookie."

"I . . . suppose we could do that," Curt says, slowly.

I lean over in my seat, and he growls, "Driving."

"I know," I whisper into his ear and slip a hand onto his crotch. He's warm and hard under his slacks.

"Guys. Guys!" Amy says, spraying crumbs.

The semi-truck misses us by a few feet.

"I'm driving!" Curt says and elbows me back to my seat. I let him do it and laugh.

"*Jenn!* What the fuck?" Amy whispers.

"Please clean up the crumbs," Curt says, his voice ragged. "Do the best job you can, Amy. Jennifer—"

"Call me Jenn, or you get another squeeze."

"Jenn. Do that again and I'm leaving you by the side of the road."

"You'd abandon me?"

"You have a phone and working fingers. You can use *Uber*."

I pull out my phone and roll down his window.

"You're bluffing," Curt tells me.

"Jenn, don't!" Amy shrieks. "She's not! She's . . . Jenn!"

"I don't bluff," I tell him.

"And I can stop the car and kick you out the second you drop that phone. It's on you if you have to walk back a few miles and find the thing while dodging traffic," Curt says.

His voice hasn't risen. It doesn't show a bit of stress.

It makes me tingle.

"What the hell is this?" I ask the air. "What . . ."

"I don't know," he says. "Just ride it out. Have patience."

"I don't, I never have, and that's the problem. Except it's not a problem, it's awesome," I say again, putting my phone down.

"You're kind of scaring me," Amy says.

"Only just now?" I ask her, grinning.

"No. Not just now."

I close my eyes.

I need Amy. I need her to be Amy, *my* Amy. She needs to live. I want to play here—I want to make Curt pull over and go after him with my nails and teeth until we're rolling in a roadside ditch, rutting, until we're naked and honest with each other and biting and fucking and dirty.

But I think I just might lose Amy if I force Curt into doing that right now.

"Sorry," I tell her. "I'll dial it back a notch."

Losing Amy is not an option. It is unacceptable.

So I keep my hands in my lap.

But no force on earth can stop me from watching him, from tracing his figure, studying his face, staring. No side-eye this time. I'm facing him while I let my imagination run wild.

And he knows what I'm doing. His breathing is different. I can see the way his cheeks have tensed up, how his gaze flicks back and forth.

The little things. The things I'm hyper-focused on.

The reactions he tries oh so desperately to hide.

He wants me.

And he knows it, now.

I don't know how he keeps calm. It fascinates me. I've never known a man with such restraint. Or a woman, for that matter.

But he doesn't crack. Not on the drive back home, not when we're in the city, heading up High Street.

Only when he turns off onto our parking lot do I see him flinch . . . and he's not looking at me.

"Uh oh, what is this?" Amy asks.

There's a whole bunch . . . a flock? A herd? A lot of police cars pulled up in the tiny parking lot behind my apartment building.

Around Chris Devon's SUV.

There are officers out cordoning the place off with yellow tape, and some serious people wearing cheap suits and sweating balls in the August humidity are talking to Becky. I see Wayne next to her, bandages wrapping his arms, wearing a *Kiss-the-cop* t-shirt and jeans. He looks absolutely mortified.

"I don't know what this is," Curt says. "Are you

comfortable if I drop you here?"

"Sure, why wouldn't I be?" I'm grinning and trying to remember if I left anything in Chris's SUV. I don't think I did.

No one even looks at me as I grab my stuff out of the back of Curt's *Camaro* and head toward the door. I swipe my card in and head to my apartment.

There's a pair of policemen in the first-floor lounge, eating donuts and chatting about how the feds suck. I ride the elevator up with a pair of guys in cheap suits and ear wires talking about how the local cops suck. Everyone gives me a glance, then a second, sizing up glance that I'm used to. No suspicion.

Once inside, I watch out the window. After a half-hour of haranguing, the guys in suits let Wayne and Becky go back inside. I glance over at the microwave and mark the time.

Sure enough, in ten minutes or so, there's a knock on my door.

I barely have enough time to get up from my couch, when Becky shoves it open and bustles in. "Oh my god, Jenn! Did you hear? Did you see that?"

"I really couldn't miss it. What happened? I was at a—"

"They found the SUV that the dead *Uber* guy drove in our parking lot! I mean, he didn't drive it in our parking lot, maybe. I mean they found it in this parking lot, somebody called because he didn't have a permit, and I bet it was Mrs. Karple who called it in, and now Wayne's been suspended pending a review, which is totally unfair because he had nothing to do with it and—" she breaks off. "Why are you pulling out that butcher knife?"

I look at it, then hide it behind my back and grin. Something in my expression makes her flinch. "Sorry, I just wanted to get some product testing done." I flip open the fridge and pull out a wrapped leg of lamb. "Do continue."

She goes on for a while, and I let her unwind. But I know what's coming, and glance at the microwave. Sure enough, five minutes later, she's bouncing up and down, and glancing towards the door. "And anyway, this is all a huge massive coincidence, and I'm sure it'll be cleared up in no time!" she bellows, already making for the door as fast as her stubby legs will carry her. The door slams behind her, and thirty seconds later, she's down the hall knocking on Lucy Hickman's door, and I hear the whole spiel start to repeat.

A Becky in motion must remain in motion. I snort laughter. In a world that was entirely random, it was comforting to have something reliable.

And oddly enough, Curt's face floated in my mind's eye.

Solid.

Reliable.

He was not my usual sort of attraction.

And yet . . .

He makes it work. Works it? Oh, definitely.

I swallow hard.

Then I head into the bathroom, strip down, and look at my wounds. I peel off band-aid after band-aid and run my fingers along the cuts and scrapes as I remember how I got them. I gasp as I push against bruises, and lick my lips as my hand strays south, down to where my legs meet.

I'm right in the middle of a really fun time when there's another knock on the door.

"What is it, Becky?" I call back.

The door opens. I jerk open the bathroom door and lean out . . . and stare at Wayne.

He stares back. Then his gaze drops south. "Well," he says.

"Something you need?" I ask. "Beyond a really good view and a restraining order?"

"Yeah, I could get that shit denied," he says, then shakes his head. "Sorry, wasn't expecting, ah . . ."

He says sorry, but he's not looking away.

"Give me a minute," I say. The buzz is gone — the memory

expunged. A Wayne does not equal a Curt, or even half or a third of a Curt. A milli-curt? No, I'm American, we don't do metric.

That makes me giggle, and he blinks in surprise, then smiles as I shut the door on him.

Two minutes later, I'm dressed, composed, and my hands are washed. And Wayne's sitting at the kitchen counter, bandaged forearms stretched out in front of him. He looks weird in a t-shirt and jeans. Not really flattering.

"You saw Becky earlier," he says, looking me up and down. Again, his gaze is drawn to my tits, even though I've got a shirt over 'em now. Should I have put on a bra? Meh. Too hot for that. I go and shut the door. It's letting my precious air conditioning escape.

"It was hard to miss Becky," I say, turning back to him. "I didn't understand everything she was saying, though. Something about some dead guy's SUV?"

"In our parking lot. For days." Wayne scowls. "The feds are trying to nail my ass to the wall, blaming me because I didn't notice it. How was I supposed to know?" He raises both hands skyward. "You ask me, Slaughterhouse did this deliberately! The guy's playing a sick game with me. Taunting me. Stalking me."

I laugh, then cover it up as a cough as he shoots me a surprised look. "Are you sure that's what's going on here?" I ask, once my *cough* is done.

"What else could it be? First, the guy tries to blow me up at his storage locker. Next, he leaves his latest victim's vehicle right next to my parking space. Oh, he's gunning for me. Not that the feds see it that way." His face twists. "The feds are saying it's an entirely different guy. Someone they call *The Watchman*. I'm pretty sure they're just making that up, though."

"Wow, uh . . . why would they do that?"

"Because they know I'm about to crack the case! I put in the work for this—I laid the groundwork, and now they'll swoop in at the last minute and grab all the glory!" He's standing now, pacing, trying to put his arms behind his back but gasping every time they bend too far. After the third time, I interrupt him.

"Hey, hey, sit down. Let me get you some chili—there's plenty left over."

"Sure. Becky'll be at least another forty minutes spreading the news. Might as well get some dinner out of it."

I reheat a bowl for him and top up a plate for myself.

And he considers me again, as he eats. "So, I'm gonna be home on administrative leave. Li'l paid vacation, y'know?"

"Nice gig if you can get it," I say. Small talk, but people expect it. Bores me, though. I'll get through this with fantasies of Curt . . .

"I wouldn't mind seeing more of you while I'm here. If you know what I mean."

That completely derails my train of thought.

I blink. He's smiling . . . no, that's a leer.

"Got a good look earlier. You didn't mind either, I could tell."

"And how would Becky feel about this?" I ask, stalling for time.

"Becky doesn't notice shit. She spends my money and goes and does a million and one little fun things with her friends. She eats out on my dime, gives me hell for coming home late, and doesn't even screw me anymore. She's always tired or has a headache, or she's on her period." He snorts. "That period runs about three weeks a month, feels like."

That's all very interesting, I'm sure, but I don't care. I've got a whole different problem.

Because now *she's* awake.

I was looking at a man earlier.

But now he's meat. He just doesn't know it yet.

"Just think it over." He leans back, smirking. "I'm packing more than a nightstick, if you know what I mean."

"I think I do," I say, and I have to fight to keep *her* from talking.

We're at home.

This is our home.

Umpteen million police and suits guys currently surround it.

This is not a place where I can safely *work*.

"I'll think it over," I say, swallowing hard and feeling my face flush. I run my tongue over my lips to catch the drool.

I'm pretty sure he thinks I'm drooling because he's hot. He's that kind of guy.

He leaves shortly after, brushing way too close to me as he goes. He gives me what he probably thinks is a smoldering wink.

And all I can think about is how well-marbled his flank is going to be when I carve him up.

CHAPTER SIXTEEN

Chaos. Chaos had infected his system.

The world was shifting—*his* world was shifting, and The Machine felt the gears in his head grinding, spinning faster, moving out of control.

And none of it made any sense.

He had done what he planned to do—hook up with Jenn, with *The Diva*, in an attempt to satisfy her urges and get her to stop obsessing over him.

Are you sure that was the only reason?

Regardless! He pushed the voice from his mind, ground it between the gears. Regardless, it hadn't helped. The Diva had demanded attention on the trip back, and it took the technical director's intervention to stop her from causing a scene.

And that was the galling part, really. The technical director had aided and abetted this liaison with long-time skill and experience handling her more impulsive friend.

It should have worked.

But he could tell, the technical director had been just as surprised as he on that drive back.

Are you really surprised? His wounds throbbed in remembrance, and he felt his cock stiffen.

She had come at him like a big cat going after a piece of meat. And fighting her off had only stoked her desire. A desire that he had to admit burned brighter than expected. His own had grown with every cut, every gash, every hit.

He.

Wanted.

Her.

And taking her, fucking her, that had only made him want her more.

The gears whirled, grinding, and he could almost taste the sparks, hot in the back of his throat.

He'd been thinking about it all the way home, turning it over and over in his mind.

Up until he'd pulled up to J—to The Diva's building, and he'd seen the array of police in their lot.

At that moment, he'd found something he hadn't expected. Acceptance.

He'd thought they were here for *him*, here to arrest The Machine. He'd thought that they had finally, finally put the pieces together. That they were hot on his trail from the storage unit, that they'd blown through the false identity he'd used to rent the thing.

But, no. They'd paid him no mind as he dropped her off. And the technical director had only made small talk as he drove her back to her own small house on the outskirts of town.

For now, it seemed that at least his secret was safe.

However, he did not believe in coincidences. The Machine could not assume that ignorance would protect him. The police might or might not be targeting Slaughterhouse, but they had crossed his path often enough that he had to protect his interests.

Fortunately, he had anticipated this problem long ago.

And with the wealth that his initial years in business had gained him, he had set up a network of eyes and ears and shell identities to keep him aware of incoming trouble.

Technology made it easy ... that, and an international mindset. And the troubles of the last few years meant that so long as his bills were paid on time, nobody looked too hard at the person who was paying them.

So The Machine reached into his briefcase, drew out the small notebook full of names and passwords, and selected an appropriate persona. This one was Larry Stane, a small-time drug dealer who had some friends who watched the FBI.

He messaged the friend who was online at the minute. Mercer was a middleman for one of the cartels down south.

Dude, what's up in Columbus?

It's been a while, Larry. Starting to think you'd caught a bullet. Hey, you remember that trade we had with Janks?

The Machine checked his notes on Larry.

What are you talking about? There wasn't any trade with Janks. It got canceled at the last minute.

I had to check. You know how it is.

The Machine did. If he'd responded the wrong way, Mercer would have erased all contact info, and someone would put down the fact that Larry was compromised. The Machine would have to drop his Larry identity forever or risk some very bad people investigating it far too deeply.

Yeah. So what's up in Columbus?

Ohio? Corn and assholes, mostly.

Yeah, but I got wind from a friend who was moving product on High Street that there was heat over there. Federales.

Let me check a few things.

The Machine pulled up his reports and started typing. *Chopco* needed a summary of the recent expenses, and his direct contact wanted a cost-benefit analysis of the last week's activity. It was light work, and he kept an eye on the text prompt as he waited. No social media messaging here, this was older stuff.

Finally, Mercer got back to him.

Nothing's affecting us directly. They're chasing down some Hannibal Lecter type asshole. International shit, but not our shit to worry about.

Oh, that's good to know. I was hoping to get some more sales in. Think you could help me supply matters?

He didn't need any of it, really. The Machine neither used nor sold drugs. But this was the price of doing business, and it reinforced his identity's cover. After it was all said and done, he'd arrange for the package to be picked up and delivered to his cover identity's door, then he'd arrange for someone to steal it off the porch and dispose of it. And Mercer wouldn't get curious so long as he got his money.

No, all of this was so he could ask one follow-up question.

You sure these feds aren't a danger to me? What's this Hannibal Lecter stuff you're talking about? I'm gonna have to reassure a few customers here, I don't want them getting nervous.

Fortunately, Mercer seemed to be feeling happy about the deal.

I'm sure. It's fucking Interpol, and it's their homicide department, not vice. There's a hotshot British detective like some fucking Sherlock Holmes wannabe tracking this guy. Word is they've been tracking this psycho for years. He's been working all over the world and icing assholes – definitely nothing at all to do with us.

That's a relief.

The Machine felt the opposite emotion well up inside him.

He *was* being hunted.

That was not the natural order of things.

The Machine concluded the transaction as expected, closed out the browser, scrubbed his Internet history, then began riffling through his notebook of identities.

He had clues to go on now. Britain. Interpol. A long-running case.

The next three identities turned up nothing.

He opened up the fourth. Lyle Stark. A friend of an elderly, somewhat confused woman whose nephew was in British Intelligence. She often forgot what she could and couldn't talk about, and though her information was questionable at best, he'd used it to conform to various business activities in the past.

And the second he did, his anti-virus software flared to life.

The Machine froze.

He ended the program instantly, deleted his Internet history . . . but not before an email popped up in Lyle's inbox.

The title read *Hello, Watchman*, and that was all The Machine had time to see before the dummy shell account he was working from closed down.

The Machine instantly turned off his laptop, then spent the next few minutes frantically using every bit of his information technology knowledge to clean it and make sure that whatever program Interpol had tried to use to trace him hadn't taken root in his system.

They had set a trap for him. He was sure of it.

The gears in his head ground and the answer came to him.

He was up against someone as orderly and troublesome as himself.

The Machine had a *nemesis*—someone who had seen the patterns within his maneuvers and lain in wait. This had been building for years, and all it had taken was something as random as his wallet card falling in the wrong place to set the whole chain in motion.

The Machine shook his head. No. This only *looked* random. There were no coincidences.

He checked once again, found his system clean. Purging worry, driving fear from his mind, he hovered his finger over the power button until he was certain he could resume his business. That this time, at least, he had escaped without any consequences.

It was a comforting thought.

And it burst like a popped balloon as someone knocked on the door.

CHAPTER SEVENTEEN

For a second, I think that I've gotten the wrong door.
Every time I take a deep breath, I feel my head pulse with excitement, even as my belly gurgles. My thoughts turn back to the dead thing walking that's named Wayne, and I gasp as my nipples harden.

I need a fix.

I need a distraction.

I need . . .

The door opens.

"I need you," I tell Curt.

He opens his mouth, and I press mine onto it, searching, finding his tongue with mine. His arms come up, and I slam into him, carrying him onto the floor of his hotel room.

He tries to catch me with his knee, and I take the hit around my belly, grunting, and whoops, almost bit my tongue! I pull back and slap him, a full-on open palm that snaps his head to the side. He grunts and straight-arms me off him.

The door clicks shut behind us.

I cut loose. I feast on him, biting wherever I can reach his skin, scrabbling for a hold to keep him down.

I try, anyway. He's not going down without a fight. He throws me around like I'm a sack of potatoes, kicks me whenever I try to get in close.

He doesn't hold back.

And he's not in his suit right now, so there's nothing hindering him.

Wait.

He's . . . oh. Oh my.

"Wow," I say as I draw back. He's naked. And glorious. And *hard*.

Curt doesn't speak, just mops blood from his lips and flicks it at me.

I laugh. "Did you undress? Just for *me*?"

When he opens his mouth, I charge him.

This is not tender.

This is nothing I ever knew I wanted before him and everything I want now.

This is pain and blood and joy and hate, and we lock eyes and know exactly what we want from each other.

A few minutes of kissing, biting, and clawing, and he pushes me back again.

"I did undress for you," Curt says, as he tests his jaw. It's not broken. "I didn't want blood all over a good set of clothes."

I laugh and skim my own shirt over my head, letting my breasts flop free. Then as he stares, I throw the shirt at his face and charge him, carrying him down to the carpet again. He's warm, so warm, and his arms wind around me like steel. I screech and try to knee him in the balls, but he turns, and my leg slides off his hip again and again as he stands and shoves me, and I fall back onto the bed. With a free hand, he goes to work on my leggings, tearing them down, and I'm warm and wet down there as his hand grabs me where my legs come together.

I gasp as the silk of my thong rides up into my vagina, and his head slams into my chest, right in my sternum, pounding above my heart. His lips find my breast, and his teeth spike into the skin, and I wrap both arms around his head and try to snap his neck.

For my troubles, I get a punch to the side of the head that makes the room swim, and before I'm recovered, his fingers are in me. I gasp again, and it takes a few tries, but I snake my hand down and find him where he's hard and throbbing.

And before he can twist away again, I have him, and he groans.

I can scarcely get my fingers around him . . . so I squeeze until I can, and he groans more.

Then I moan as I feel his fingers hook inside me, feel the rubbing turn into a spike as his fingernails graze.

He's giving me cuts up *there.*

And the thought makes me swell and flicker and rock on the bed as I come so hard that his fingers slip from me, but I don't care because I've let go of him to grab the bed as I whine my rapture to his face, inches away.

Then he's up and on me and over me, and his warmth, his bloody warmth is wrapping me in two strong arms, and that glorious length is sliding up my thigh, catching me just as my muscles go slack and loose.

He stretches me to fullness, and I wrap bloody hands around his hips and push him up until I can take no more of him, and we are joined in whatever the hell this unholy mess we've made is called.

It's a connection.

Mutually assured destruction?

Maybe.

He moves then, and I pant. He palms one breast and squeezes until I let go of his hips to try and fend him off. Then he slides back, and I gasp as he goes, feel the warmth flare and the wet flow as I hunger to feel him again, and he feeds himself slllloooooowwwwwly back in, punctuating each inch or so with a twist of my nipple as he holds me down.

I howl, and my fist catches his throat.

He coughs, collapses on me, and for a second, I think I've killed him, but I don't care because he'll stay hard a while longer, warm a while longer, and I shove him to the side, straddle him as he coughs. His member is slick with my juices and our blood, and I grab this idol of my joy and slide my hand up and down to make sure I've got his attention, sliding the skin against the cartilage, making him groan even through a bruised throat.

Then I hop up his legs, twist his manhood until it's juuuuusssst piercing my lips, and lower myself down, squeezing him with each muscle as I go.

I'm on top now.

He's *mine*.

I have his arms pinned for a second, but he catches my ass with a knee from behind, and I yelp and slip forward, off him.

For a second, I feel loss, terrible loss . . . but he's got me again, grabbing me by the waist and lifting me up . . . up to slide down upon him.

Impaled.

Full.

Warm, and oh, oh, there's another one, and this one's stronger, more violent . . . but I'm on top of him now — I'm holding his member solid inside me, like a knife pierced to the hilt in a roast, and it has nowhere to go.

And after the third wave, after I'm clamped down tight and feeling every vein under his man's flesh, I feel him pulse within me. I feel wetness and know that it's not more of my own, as he unleashes his seed within me.

I can almost feel my womb open to him, drawing the essence of him in, drinking him.

Then I collapse on top of him, still joined, the sheets sticky and red and shining with sweat and more.

There's no sound for a while, no sound save for panting from me, and heavy breathing from him.

From Curt.

He's still inside me. Softening now, but still filling me . . . enough . . . for now.

"I don't know what it is we've got here," I tell him.

"Death for at least one of us if we keep it up," he rasps.

I laugh.

"Still worth it," I whisper back. "Either way it goes."

"It is, isn't it? It feels . . . right. And I don't know why," he tells me.

"I don't either."

"I want to know."

I shrug. "Why? It just is. Enjoy it."

He breathes, and I ride the wave of his body up.

I giggle and then sigh in disappointment as he finally slips from me, flaccid and oozing.

"I've got a lot on my mind. Most of it's about you," he tells me. "I'm . . . I don't think this can be a long-term . . . thing."

"I want more," I tell him, staring into his eyes from an inch away, watching them smolder. "And so do you."

"I *do*," he groans. "But . . . I have work. I have very, very important work."

"You're more than your job," I tell him, and he flinches as I lift a hand. But I caress his face, trace the stubble on his chin.

"I thought I was my job. I thought my work was every-thing." He closes his eyes. "I don't think I can give it up."

"Want me to give up mine?" I say. "It's fun, but it's not my life. It's not what I really want to do."

"You're good at it, though. You bring the numbers. It . . ." He frowns. "It feels *right* for you." Then he blinks. "Did you just ask to move in with me or something like that?"

He gasps as my hand finds his penis, and I give him a few pumps. "Something like that," I whisper into his ear.

We fuck again, a little less painful this time. It's a tired sort of sex, slow and heavy and sweet like a good pudding.

I could see myself with him. "But I've got my own prob-lems," I say, lying next to him and with his arm over me like a shield on a knight's arm.

"Problems . . ." he says drowsily. Then he snaps awake. "Do you? I thought you didn't worry about . . . anything, really."

"It's Wayne. He wants to fuck me."

Instantly I feel him stiffen. His eyes harden up, gone from a dopey, sleep-craving haze to something harder than steel, with cold anger deep down inside.

I stare into them, mesmerized.

This is Curt. This is who he really is.

"You're talking about the detective," Curt says, after a moment.

"Yes," I whisper, sitting up from him, still working his shaft. He's halfway there, stiffening.

"He's married," Curt says, and there's an edge to his voice.

"I know," I say, and I smile as I think of how I'll open him up and find every good cut inside him. "And I want him. That's why I'm here, to forget about how I want him so *bad*—"

And suddenly I'm up against the wall, with pain in my back, gasping.

I look down to his hand on my shoulder, white-knuckled. It hurts, and I gasp. I see down to his member, dripping with blood where my nails caught it.

It must hurt like the devil, but he's glaring at me, staring at me with a cold fury rolling from him like the dead of winter.

"Oh my God," I whisper and giggle. "This . . . you're beautiful."

"Get. Out." His voice makes the inside of my skull throb.

"I . . ."

"Bathroom. Wash up. Get your clothes on. Go," he grinds out.

"I . . . yes," I whisper.

He wants to kill me now.

And oh, I feel myself loosening again, feel my labia

warming and spreading.

But I go into the bathroom and start the shower.

I wonder if he'll be there when I get out. A weaker man would flee his own room. I resolve to trash it if he has.

But I don't think he has.

He's got courage, Curt does. He'll be there when I leave. He's sturdy. Reliable. Inhumanly so. Like a thing of . . . oh, what is it? Something trustworthy. Something metal.

Maybe he *will* try to kill me. I laugh at the thought.

Oh, I'm sore. And the water feels so good.

To my complete lack of surprise, there's a mostly unused pack of bandages and an assortment of disinfectants on the counter. It looks like I wasn't the only one patching myself back up recently.

Curt's waiting when I get out and tapping away at his laptop. He's dressed and pointing to something on the bed.

It's a small, bronze-colored disk.

"What's this?" I ask him.

"A gift," he says simply. "Remember me when you're fucking Wayne."

I want to protest, want to say that wasn't what I meant, but . . . how would I even begin to explain it?

He wouldn't understand.

And I hate him, just a bit, for that.

I take the disk. It's got some weight to it and a clasp on the front. Too big for a medallion, even though there's a fob for a chain.

"It's a watch," he says simply.

I shake my head and turn to leave . . . but I give him one last look as I go.

His face is stone. His eyes are steel.

"A watch," I say, as I study him. Reliable. Metal. Constant like the watch. Like its . . ."Gears," I breathe.

He flinches then, surprised — his jaw drops.

And I shut the door behind me.

Midway down the elevator, I sag against the wall, tired in mind to match my body.

I had gotten Wayne out of my mind. I had exhausted *her*, distracted *her*. Kept *her* from doing something truly stupid — for now.

But at the cost of alienating Curt.

I'd fucked up.

Badly.

And now anything that might have been, anything we could have been, that was gone.

Forever.

CHAPTER EIGHTEEN

It's not forever, Curt," Randall said, his voice echoing in the phone's speaker.

"It's close enough," The Machine grumbled, as he sat on the one unstained bed left in his hotel room and cleaned his wounds.

"It's a week. Two more shows."

"And one of us will be dead by the end of it."

"You're usually not one to exaggerate."

"I wish I was," The Machine told him, rotating his neck and hearing vertebrae click.

"She really got under your skin, huh?"

"Big time," The Machine confirmed, as he tacked a band-aid onto his chest. "Though I'm pretty sure it's mutual."

"Curt. *Chopco* is *happy*. The numbers are huge. And have you checked the comments on the streams?"

"No. Why? Has there been a significant data shift recently?" The Machine frowned.

"Just have a look."

The Machine pulled up the latest video. The technical director had titled it *Making Whoopie*.

And the comments were . . . enlightening.

"Half of these comments are asking questions about me," The Machine said, slowly.

"Yeah."

"They're wondering if I'm Jenn's boyfriend." Only when he said it out loud did he realize that he'd said Jenn and not *The Diva*.

Even his thoughts were no refuge from her!

"Yeah. In two episodes, you brought some drama to this show."

"Have you seen the stream? There was plenty of drama here before my arrival," The Machine told him.

"Yeah. But there's no drama like a potential romantic drama. You and her, you've got chemistry. Or at least it looks that way onscreen."

"Chemistry. Like nitro and glycerin," The Machine told him.

"I'm pretty sure that's not how you make nitroglycerin."

"There are explosions regardless." The Machine looked at the deep scratches on the back of his hand. Then he gritted his teeth and poured hydrogen peroxide over the scabs.

"Hey? Didn't catch that last part. You okay?"

"I'm fine," The Machine said tightly. "I fell down some stairs earlier."

"Ouch. But listen, whatever you're doing, no matter how hard it is, it's working. And giving up now . . . well, you know your reputation."

"I do," The Machine ground out.

He didn't give up.

That was what allowed him to take the jobs he chose and charge the prices he did. If he gave up here over personal reasons, then it would be a crack in his facade. A flaw in the structure that he had built, steadily, year after year.

"My direct, onscreen presence is beneficial, according to these indicators."

"Yeah. You're doing too good a job to quit."

"Am I? Are you certain it's me? Or is this merely riding the wave of the dead raccoon fiasco?" The Machine asked.

Randall sighed. "Honestly, I don't know. You think you're a flash in the pan?"

"I think we need more analysis before we reach a final

decision here," The Machine said. "How are negotiations with *Buca di Beppo* going?"

"Great. The last show helped immensely, and the undeniable spike in *Chopco* orders gave me the ammunition I needed. They're sold. I notified Amy — she's setting up for a show this coming Friday. So you lost a week, but no big deal."

"Five days. That should give us some time to heal," The Machine muttered.

"What?"

"Nothing." The Machine weighed his options, decided the risk was minimal. "I'll be moving out of the hotel. I've found an apartment elsewhere."

"What? Now? Mid-job? This is new. You feeling all right?"

"I am. But this recent stress is causing some unease. I'm going to need more open space before I feel I'm working to my best efficiency."

"Normally, you ask me to handle booking new places."

"Fortunately, I'm in-country and local enough to know my options. I didn't need your assistance with avoiding problems. Don't get me wrong," The Machine said, as he realized that his comment might be unacceptable to normal people. "I still value your expertise and skills. But in this case, it was a minor chore at worst."

"All right, all right. Just remember I'm here if you need anything. I'm your Amy if it comes down to it."

"Who?"

"Jesus, you're bad with names. Amy Buller? The technical director? The other lady you've been working with the last week or so?"

"Ah, yes, her. She's very competent."

"She's pretty much the show. Everything but the star, anyway."

Gears whirred to life in The Machine's mind.

Possibilities opened up.

And he gave them a good, hard look.

"Hello? You still there?"

"I am."

The rest of the conversation was short and covered a few minor matters. He bandaged as he went, and after Randall was done, The Machine hung up and began the slow process of scrubbing away the obvious bloodstains throughout the room.

The other stains he left in place. It was a hotel room, after all. The staff had seen worse.

Then he simply packed up and left. He handled everything related to the checkout online, tallied his reward points, and made his way to the parking garage.

It was only a short drive north, up to Sawmill Road, and a rented *Airbnb* in a quiet neighborhood up against some woods. He had rented the three nearest properties under different names, but he only truly needed one. The others were just to prevent anyone from hearing anything suspicious. He leaned back in his car seat and went through the check-in process online. In short order, he received the code for the lockbox on the front door and was exploring the place. Simple, two-storied, and four-bedroomed, it had enough space for what he needed.

It would be space enough to kill The Diva without anyone knowing.

It was the only way.

It was the logical thing to do.

She was an avatar of chaos! A fickle and unpredictable creature. Once his time with the show was done, she could die, and he would be gone. He could ensure that her body was never found, and given her erratic nature, everyone would probably think she had fled on a whim.

Jenn deserved it.

She was a selfish, foolish, thing who . . . and The Machine

realized that he'd just thought of her by name again.

No.

She was The Diva. *The Diva!*

There, in the barely furnished living room, The Machine sank to the floor and clutched his head.

She had to die for him to stay who he was.

That was the truth of it.

She was getting inside his mind, getting into the gears. Threatening everything he'd built, threatening his *work*.

And yet . . .

And yet, he wanted her.

He had felt complete inside her, had felt peace when she lay next to him, their blood mingling.

He had felt a peace he hadn't expected to feel until he was dead.

"She needs to die," he whispered. "Or I will never be free."

CHAPTER NINETEEN

"It can't be free!" I tell Amy.

"It is. Every ingredient is free. Using their kitchen? Free. And what's more? They are actually gonna close the restaurant down to the public and only allow ticket holders in while this is going on."

"Wow," I whisper. "How?"

"Curt. And his friend Randall. I don't know what they did, but *Buca di Beppo* is bending over sideways to give us everything we need for this." Amy grinned. "I'm thinking of chicken parmigiana for this one."

"I don't know, that's pretty simple." I chew my lip. "Veal parmigiana?"

"Some people get weird about eating calves."

"Would it piss off *PETA*?"

"Totally."

"Worth it. Veal parmigiana it is."

"Why are we picking fights with *PETA* again?"

"They came at *us*, Amy. Over a raccoon. Wasn't even a domesticated raccoon!"

"I don't think you can domesticate raccoons."

"Semantics." I think that's the word—the word for saying that how you say words is less important than what you mean.

"Okay, okay. I'll let them know that veal's the dish du jour."

"Cool. I'll give Curt a call and let him know the plans."

And on my way back home, it occurs to me that's a lie.

160

I won't call him.

I've called him three times since that night I jumped him in his hotel room, and the phone keeps telling me that number is no longer in service.

I'm not going to call him.

I'm going to go see him.

Three minutes later, I'm parked in my lot and jogging over to his hotel.

Seven minutes later, I'm at his door.

I pound on it like a madwoman, and a muffled voice tells me to go away.

I pound some more. He can't hide from me! He can't deny what we had!

"You *liar!*" I scream.

The door cracks open, and I throw myself against it. There's the snap of a chain and I'm on him, burying my teeth in his cheek and . . . and someone's screaming in my ear.

And he's a hell of a lot flabbier than I remember.

And . . . it isn't him.

I pull my teeth out of the guy's face and stare down at a middle-aged man wriggling under me. He's half-dressed, and there's a pair of broken spectacles over some watery, fearful eyes.

"Oh my god, did you not order the love bites?" I say.

"What?" he gasped.

"This is room eleven-oh-nine, right?"

"This is the seventh floor!"

"Shit, sorry, wrong room. My bad. Don't worry. My company will cover it. I'll just go . . . call them . . ."

I'm out the door, and I run for all I'm worth.

Two security guards jog towards me, and I slow. "Thank god!" I tell them, forcing tears. "He attacked me! He's back there!" I point backward, and they take off, looking angry.

Well, that was embarrassing.

There's a lot of yelling, and Mister Room Rando screaming about how I bit his face, but the elevator doors close, and I leave before anyone can stop me.

And once I'm out and the adrenaline is ebbing away, I mop my face and feel the tears stinging behind my eyes.

He ghosted me.

We had something. We had the . . . he was the only one I could ever *do* that with.

It wasn't sex. Well, it was that, too, but it was *more*.

I don't know what it was.

It wasn't . . . it wasn't love. I don't think. I don't think I can love, can care about someone more than myself. I'm broken that way. But this . . . it was more. Different. Stronger.

I've never felt anything like that. And I want to feel it again and again until we're both raw and bloody heaps of meat and bones. I want to hurt him and be hurt until our nerves are burnt remnants, and we can't feel anything else.

I need him.

Once I'm back in my apartment and cleaned up, I call him again. And again, the number's out of service.

I want to shove my phone down the garbage disposal.

Instead, I text Amy.

I tried to call him, and he's not picking up.

Really? Let me try.

It won't work, his number's out of service.

So I'll message him.

Oh! I forgot I could do that!

I go looking for him on social media, and . . . he's a ghost.

There is no sign of him on *Facebook*, nothing on *Instagram* or *Twitter*. I even check *TikTok*, in case he has a fetish for singing in the shower or something.

Spoilers—he doesn't. At least not on *TikTok*.

I'm sitting there wondering what to do when I notice Amy's message box is flashing.

So, I let him know what's going on, but I've got some bad news.

Yeah?

He's feeling sick. He's going to try to get over it, but he might have to stay away from the show on Friday.

"No! He can't! Don't you *run* from me, Curt!"

It takes me a second to realize that I said that out loud, instead of typing it.

He can't!

Amy is annoying logical.

He can. It's in his contract that personal attendance isn't mandatory. And honestly, if he's sick, I don't want him to give me anything.

He's not. He's lying.

Jenn . . . Is this a Brett thing?

I haven't thought about Brett in years. Brett cheated on me. Now when I think about Brett, all I remember is sitting on his chest, looking at him through *her* eyes as his blood sprays all over my skin.

No. Not a Brett thing. Yet. But the night's pretty fucking young.

It's the middle of the day.

Semantics!

Jenn, you've known him for a week or so. You had one hook-up.

Two.

Shit, should I have typed that?

Oh. Oh . . .

What?

I'm guessing you called *him* on *that second hookup.*

It kinda worked out that way — sort of.

Jenn. You can be intense. You know that.

So what do you want me to do? We have something. We do. He's just . . .

I pause. I don't have the words, really.

But Amy does.

You haven't lost him yet, Jenn. But you will if you push too hard. Give it some time. Play it cool. If you want him, you have to come on less strong.

But —

No.

I want to —

No, Jenn.

I contemplate killing her. Then my mind shuts down in horror. No! That's *Amy.*

And I type the hardest words I've ever typed.

You're right. I'll try.

And I do.

The next few days are agony. I can barely get out of bed. I keep myself busy by hunting for him on social media. But he's nowhere to be found.

This is bizarre. I mean, he's a business guy! He should at least be on *LinkedIn*!

I make a note to mention it to him after we break the next bed we end up on. It's really unprofessional!

Friday comes, and I have not. I have heard nothing from Curt. And every time I pester Amy, she gets shorter and shorter with me.

Curter.

Heh.

I'm a mess. But . . . the show must go on. And I'll see him. Soon.

I know it.

He isn't a coward, after all.

He's just . . .

I don't finish the thought. But it plays in my mind all the way on the drive over to *Buca di Beppo's.*

The parking lot is mostly empty. There's an hour to go before the show. Still, some fans are lined up near the main entrance, and I see people waving and holding up phones. Their cheers echo across the lot, and I wave back, then run toward the staff entrance. Or what I think is the staff entrance. It takes a little pounding and running around the back of the building before I find a door that Amy opens.

Inside, the restaurant is set up like an old-style house—not too many corridors, mostly rooms that connect together. It's close, and the decoration looks like Italy exploded all over the walls. The long-soaked-in odor of garlic and tomato sauce inundate the place, and I can feel my waistline growing with every carb-soaked breath.

Amy introduces me to the manager, but I barely register his face, let alone his name. And the moment he's gone, I turn to her and whisper, "Where is he?"

Amy sighs. "I knew this would happen. Look, he'll show, or he won't. Just calm down. Spin the pope head a few times."

I'm a wreck right now, but that still makes me blink. "The what?"

"One of the customer booths has a bust of the pope in the center of the table on a revolving thingy. You can spin it to glare at people."

That distracts me for all of two minutes, as I see just how fast I can spin the pope head.

But then anger fills me. He's not coming. *He's not coming!*

I stomp over to my bag, angrily root around for my phone . . . and *she* slides out, falling onto the table.

I pause.

When did I pack *her* face?

Why did I pack *her* face?

Because you know how this ends, *she* whispers in my ear. You know he's *mine*.

"Jenn?" Amy asks.

I look up from the butcher knife embedded in the shattered remnants of the pope head in its case.

"Yeah?"

"Jenn! Oh my god!" She rushes over to try and clean things up, and I stuff *her* face back in my bag. And as I do so, I see there's a message on my phone.

My heart skips a beat.

It's from CC. And there's no doubt in my mind who CC is.

"Jenn, I don't know what to say," Amy wails on behind me. "Stay here. I'll get a mop. Oh God. It's like ten minutes to showtime!"

It's like a buzzing in my ears. I open the message and read two words.

Look outside.

I grab my bag and flee outside.

I don't see him, not immediately. But there's a crowd, and they're around my car.

For a second, I think I'm being carjacked, and my hand slides down to my bag and closes around the hilt of a butcher knife.

Then the crowd cheers and parts, and I see what they've done to my little car.

It's ribbons and chalk and hearts, and they've done it up like I'm getting married.

They love me. And for a second, just a second, I forget the breakdown I'm having and pump my fist in the air, and the crowd roars, and a large figure with two bandaged forearms steps out of the lines and ambles toward me. "Hey," Wayne Button says, grinning.

And instantly, I realize my prey has come to me.

Right when I can barely think straight.

Right in the middle of a huge crowd, with witnesses recording me.

"What the fuck are you doing here!" I scream and back up.

He looks surprised, and so does the crowd. Cheering dissolves into a puzzled rumble. There are hundreds of people out here, more than could fit in the restaurant, and they're confused.

"That Curt guy told me to come here and tell you to check the time," the meat named Wayne says. "Why? What's wrong?"

The time!

I rummage in my bag and pull out the little brass watch he gave me! Distantly I see people lifting phones high to focus on me as I pop open the timepiece.

There's a scrap of paper in there—an address on Sawmill Road.

My head feels like it's going to explode, and I hear *her* whisper from the bag.

She tells me *he* set this up.

She tells me *he's* waiting.

She tells me I need to go there, or *he'll* be lost to me forever!

I'm in my car before I can second guess myself, tossing my bag in the back.

I nearly run over Wayne on the way out, and the crowd parts for me as he chases after my car. But I don't care.

I have an address.

I know where he's hiding! I pull the paper out, nearly cause a wreck as I type the address on the phone and Siri tells me where to go. Something metal is rattling in back, and I think my fans tied cans or knives or something to some of the ribbons, but I can't say.

Police sirens in the distance. I don't care. I am beyond caring.

There are lights a few cars back behind me at one point, so I floor it on the highway and peel past. I take the exit to Sawmill Road, and I think they get tangled in traffic. Siri on *Google* guides me, and before long, I'm pulling up to a two-story house off in a little cul-de-sac.

The garage door's open, and I drive in, slam against the opposite wall. The garage door starts clunking down behind me, and I catch a flash of movement as the door into the house slams shut.

"*Curt!*" I yell, and I can barely see I'm so angry at his stupid little games, so frustrated, and so . . . so . . .

So wet.

So very wet.

He's here.

We're going to rip each other to little pieces, fucking our way down to hell.

CHAPTER TWENTY

"Curt!"

The Machine nodded as she yelled. He put down the garage door opener and flicked the switch to the soundboard.

It had taken a day to install cameras and intercoms in every room, including the garage. He had a good view on his laptop as she swore and tried to break down the door, varying curses with incoherent screaming.

Now he pushed the button that brought the intercom to life. "Welcome, Diva."

"Who?" She threw her shoulder into the door again, and The Machine felt satisfaction that it still held. He'd reinforced it well.

Behind her, in the camera, her car stood defaced with graffiti and twine. The Machine had no idea why, but he felt no real surprise.

It was Jenn, after all. Weird stuff happened.

No! No, she was *The Diva*.

The Machine snarled in frustration. He needed his mind on matters, needed to focus.

"I'm opening the door," he said through the intercom. "Come and find me. And together, we shall figure out what is wrong within you. We'll fix you."

And the gears hummed to life in his brain, moving so quickly that he gasped in joy. He felt himself throb to life, felt his cock rise, and strain against his pants.

He'd never had *this* reaction before. It had never been sexual before.

The Machine felt a sliver of uncertainty but pushed it away. He looked down at the workbench, next to his laptop. To the cloth mask with the glittering watch components sewn into it, the interlocking weave of metal against black cloth, glittering in the dim light that filtered through the closed windows.

Then he tapped in a quick command on his laptop and watched the door from the garage open.

The Diva didn't immediately go through. She stopped, staring at it, and The Machine hesitated. The gears skipped a beat.

The Diva marched back to her car, hauled out her over-sized purse, then booted the door aside and strode into the kitchen.

The gears clicked into place again, and The Machine felt satisfaction. This would go as he had planned. She would move from room to room, testing doors, finding some locked, and others open. And eventually, she would find her way downstairs, where —

The outer alarm beeped.

The Machine moved to the outer security cameras.

There was a car pulled up on the curb — a black sedan. And two men getting out, wearing good suits. One of them had curly brown hair and was pointing up at the house, smiling.

The other was a stocky, mustached man currently racking shells into a pump-action shotgun.

The Machine's felt his gears grind. *Too soon!* How had they tracked him this soon?

Behind them, he could see police cars on the road, pulling in. The pair turned, and the outer microphones caught a snippet of conversation.

"Locals got here early. Best get a leg on."

The one spoke with a British accent.

And The Machine *knew*.

This was the hotshot detective. This was Interpol.

This was his nemesis.

An earth-shattering crash from below and The Machine hurried over to the laptop. He realized he'd taken his focus off of his prey!

The Machine flicked through the cameras downstairs.

Half of them were out.

This gave him pause. A technical malfunction?

He switched over to the downstairs study. That one worked.

Then there was a blur of motion. Something swung toward the camera, and the screen went dark.

She was destroying the cameras!

The gears in his brain stuttered. And when he looked back to the outside cameras, two of them were dark as well.

Things were rapidly spiraling out of control. He needed . . .

The basement stair alarm tripped, and The Machine sighed in relief.

Jenn — *The Diva* had entered the last chamber.

He grabbed his mask and hurried downstairs.

It might be the last thing he would ever do, but he would fix her. He would do this one last thing for the world before he was caught or killed.

Down the back stairs then, unlocking doors as he went. He grabbed his tool bag from the counter and opened the door to the pantry.

The basement door loomed, open into darkness. In the distance, down below, he could hear shelves and glass being thrown around as she searched for him.

The Machine took a deep breath . . . and the door behind him clicked open.

"Do not move," a clipped voice said in a British accent.

The Machine froze. "How?" he asked.

"You were clever. But I specialize in patterns. Analysis. And you've been my hobby for the last three years. Turn around slowly."

The Machine turned. The man he'd seen out front, the curly-haired one in the suit, was smiling at him. The pistol in his hand was pointed squarely at The Machine's heart.

"How are you *here?*" The Machine asked. His voice held no particular emotion. Nor did his heart. He felt . . . empty.

"The watch was a clever maneuver. You meant to throw me off track, make me assume that she was The Watchman. Then she would disappear. We would hunt for her and find nothing, and you'd be free to slip the net. Is that an accurate summary of your plans?"

"It is," The Machine conceded. He'd known that the watch would get noticed sooner or later. But so soon? "But how are you here *now?*"

"Because she's loved, you soulless thing," the detective sneered. "Something a creature like you will never understand. Her fans decorated her vehicle, and the police were able to track it easily. They're right behind me, as it happens. But I'm the one to make the arrest. You're under my jurisdiction, Watchman."

"That's not my name," The Machine told him.

"It doesn't matter. I've out-thought you every step of the way. You're predictable. You love your patterns. We'll have plenty of time to interrogate you in custody, if names matter so much to you."

And from behind him, he heard feet on the stairs, pounding up the stairs.

"Ah, there you are, miss," the detective said, glancing over briefly. "You're safe now. Just stay calm and *bloody hell!*"

The detective backpedaled.

Something struck The Machine's side, knocking him away.

The gunshot echoed, and something he knew was a bullet cut the air where The Machine had been standing.

And then the detective screamed.

The Machine rolled up to his hands and knees and stared.

She was naked, and the fresh blood dripped from her creamy skin, over the bruises and tears he'd given her nights ago. Naked save for her head. There was something brown on there, brown and cracked and weathered that covered her head, with stitches, heavy cord stitches crossing it like a baseball's cover.

She was hunched over the detective, head pressed to his chest, moving to either side, and it took him a second to realize what he was seeing.

Then blood sprayed up in a fountain, and he realized.

And the gears clicked together, as he *understood.*

"Slaughterhouse," he breathed, as he heard feet on the back stoop, and a door exploded inward. "You're Slaughterhouse."

The masked head lifted.

And from the skins of her past victims, from the stitched mass of bloody flesh, two furious eyes caught his.

The Machine turned then and fled downstairs. He needed to think. And with lightning speed, with cold efficiency, his gears churned and whirled and told him what he must do.

He fled down into the basement, feet crinkling on the plastic tarps, through the smashed doorways as he heard pursuit behind him. He fled to the place where he'd stashed an emergency knife and slid it into his pocket. Then he ripped at his clothes, tearing them half off, ripped at his skin to make it bleed.

Only then did he take out his own mask. Only then did he put it on, feeling the metal scrape his skin through the cloth, felt the gears settle around him on the outside, to match the inside.

Only then was he complete.

Footsteps upstairs, shouting, but he could hear her naked feet padding below, just now hitting the plastic wrap. She'd come down here just in time.

As feet pounded on the stairs, a distant, familiar voice shouted, "Leave it to me! This is my collar!"

But The Machine stepped out from the shadows, stepped out as *she* entered the last doorway.

A mask of flesh looked upon a mask of gears.

"I understand you now," The Machine said, his voice cold as arctic wind. "I understand why you were drawn to me."

"And you to *me*." Her voice was low, guttural, something dead in a well for days decomposing. Naked but for a cloak of blood, with a knife in one hand and the detective's head in the other.

And that was all The Machine had time to see, as a blur of motion barreled into her from behind.

"Got you!" Wayne Button cheered as he tackled Jenn to the ground. She screeched like a cat and fought, but click went handcuffs, and Wayne had her in a stranglehold. "God! I can't believe I was this blind! You were right in front of me this whole time, *Slaughterhouse!*"

She fought.

She bit.

She screamed.

But Wayne had her in a hold, and The Machine could see it was a good one.

"High school wrestling champ of Ninety-three, baby!" Wayne crooned. "Now stop wiggling that cute ass and settle down. You're *mine.*"

Those words.

Those words filled The Machine with rage, fury he thought he was immune to.

"No," he said.

Wayne looked up. "Curt! Man, you okay? Looks like she did a number on . . . wait. What the hell are you wearing?"

And that decided it. The gears ground their cruel arithmetic and gave him a new answer.

The Machine moved forward and, with smooth efficiency, took his knife and killed Wayne Button.

Jenn—no, Slaughterhouse—froze under him as Wayne gurgled, and new blood flowed down to coat her. Then her eyes opened wide and puzzled as The Machine rolled over, still holding Wayne's dying body, mock wrestling with it.

He looked over into her shocked eyes. "Get your mask off and put it on him."

There was understanding then—understanding and glee.

The Machine dealt with his own mask, stuffed it into Wayne's pocket. Then he grabbed Slaughterhouse's naked form, led her over to the corner, and held firmly to the knife. "Cry," he commanded her.

She wailed like a banshee, right into his ear, and he barely managed to restrain himself from stabbing her.

And as feet pounded on the stairs and panicked policeman called to each other, The Machine closed his eyes and pretended to shake with adrenaline.

This would work, or it wouldn't.

Although, now that he thought of it, there was one last little detail to take care of.

"Here's the story we need to tell them . . ." he whispered to the beautiful, twisted, apex predator in his arms.

CHAPTER TWENTY-ONE

I'm sitting here on the beach, under the Honduran sun, with a Mai Tai in my hand, a bikini over my bits, and my phone showing me the latest headlines from back home.

Slaughterhouse Shut Down! One big headline reads.

Murder Mansion on the Market for Millions! Another reads.

Star Of Popular Cooking Show Narrowly Escapes Being Dish Du Jour! That one is my favorite so far.

I'm sitting here on my little beach blanket — *Versace* — wearing a bikini that costs more than two months of rent at my old apartment — *Gucci* — and sipping sweet drinks under a sun I never expected to see from this angle.

It was all so easy.

She expected us to be caught, finally.

She expected to die in that basement, shot to bits.

She didn't care, so long as she took Curt with her, as long as she killed that *liar*.

But.

Now I know. Now we know.

There is no Curt.

There's only The Machine.

And I look over to him, that smooth mound of man-flesh, his wounds bandaged over from our last lovemaking.

We're learning the boundaries now, learning to take it slow, to fuck without serious damage.

We still hurt. We still bleed. We still gouge and tear. But we do it within limits because now we have each other forever.

Or until we're finally caught—until we finally die.

Or maybe . . . maybe we'll turn on each other at some point. Maybe one of us will grow weak, or lose their way, or slip headlong into madness.

The prospect excites me, and I nuzzle up to him. He grunts but turns slightly, rolls, and puts an arm around me. I'm sheltered in his frame, and I don't want to eat him. He's not meat. He's The Machine.

My Machine.

"Are you really working right now?" I ask as I see him sneak his phone back into our beach bag.

"In a way. Regardless of how much the Columbus PD believes that Wayne Button was Slaughterhouse, Interpol probably isn't sold on the idea that he was also their *Watchman*. I'm doing what I can to defray matters there. It's taking time and resources."

"Boring." I yawn. When I open my eyes again, I catch his smoldering gaze tracking my lips. I give them a long lick and feel him shudder. He's hard against me now, two thin layers of cloth separating us from joining.

"Boring to you," he says. "Frankly, I'm still not sure how the hell you avoided being caught for so long."

"Just lucky, I guess."

"I don't believe in luck. Well, I didn't," he says, as he rolls back over again. "It helped that Wayne had a history of sneaking out on his wife, and some of those liaisons coincided with Slaughterhouse's murders. And that the rest of his task force didn't like him to begin with."

"Amy says hi, by the way," I purr into his ear.

"Oh, you're keeping touch? Good. How is she doing?"

"Working with *Chopco* on the relaunch. The funding stream got approval, and now she's putting together a good crew, and making the first calls out for venues. You should see her. She's busy as a one-legged man at an ass-kicking contest and twice as happy."

"I wasn't aware ass-kicking contests were happy places," My Machine says, and his lips turn up, just a bit.

"Is that a *smile*? Actual emotion?" I tickle him.

He almost breaks my fingers as he slaps them away, and I laugh. Sweet, sweet pain!

"So, anyway, the show's gonna be there when I get back," I tell him. "Bigger and better than ever."

"Good," is his one-word reply.

We're quiet for a bit then.

"Am I going to have to stop hunting?" I ask him. "I don't know if I can. I don't know how. *She* won't let me."

"I can't imagine what it's like to have that problem," My Machine says. "But no, we don't have to stop. In fact . . ."

He rolls the other way, reaches into the bag, and draws out a small box, about the size for . . .

No.

Way.

"Are you serious?" I ask, and my voice breaks.

He pops it open.

There are two rings inside. One's pure gold. The other is glistening with rubies and diamonds, crawling in a pattern that looks like gristle and bloody flesh.

And I get it immediately. One's for me. One's for *her*.

I squeal and throw myself on him, kissing him over and over again.

And if *she* takes the opportunity to rake bloody furrows into his biceps, well, that's okay.

"We'll find them together," he says, his voice cold under the warm sun. "The cheaters, the crooks, the ones who make the world worse. We'll find them, and we'll end them together. Yes?"

"Yes," I whisper back, my voice raw and husky.

This is great!

Actually being married will make hunting meals down so much easier!

And I lie there in the arms of my man—no.

Not my man.

My Machine.

ABOUT THE AUTHOR

Myra Flexion has alibis for everything. You can prove nothing.